MYSTERY AT THE FAIRGROUNDS

DEDICATION

For June Varnum, Judy Morrow
and Robin Jones Gunn,
who are my true writing friends,
and for all my dear writing prayer partners

ACKNOWLEDGMENTS

Many thanks to Linda Mangham
for advice on cat-raising
And also to Plumas-
Sierra County Fair officials and volunteers
in Quincy, California, for providing
such a beautiful setting.

MYSTERY AT THE FAIRGROUNDS

JANET HOLM MCHENRY

Chariot VICTOR
PUBLISHING
A DIVISION OF COOK COMMUNICATIONS

ANNIE SHEPARD MYSTERIES
Mystery at the Fairgrounds
Secret of the Locked Trunk
Mystery at the Old Stamp Mill

Designer: Andrea Boven
Cover Illustration: Rick Johnson

CIP information available upon request.

2 3 4 5 6 7 8 9 10 01 00 99 98 97

Chariot Books is an imprint of ChariotVictor Publishing,
a division of Cook Communications, Colorado Springs, Colorado 80918
Cook Communications, Paris, Ontario
Kingsway Communications, Eastbourne, England

CONTENTS

FIRE AND LIGHTS

I kicked the smoldering log in the makeshift campfire pit. "See, guys, it's just like I told you. What do you think?"

"Oh, I don't know, Annie," said Maria, flipping back her dark long permed hair. "What's the big deal anyway? It's just a campfire."

"Each night when I look out my bedroom window...see it? It's that white house right over there up the hill a ways. Anyway, each night I see this little campfire here on the back side of the county fairgrounds. I don't think the maintenance man knows because it's behind the grandstand. And each morning when I rush out here, there's no one here."

"Maybe it's somebody camping out or just having fun," said Alia, biting her nails. She teetered on a stone and looked me straight in the eye. "High school kids do stuff like that here. It's safe at night—not like in the big city."

"I wonder...." I picked up my backpack, heavy with books.

"I wonder where my Chevy is tonight...." Maria and Alia sang nasally in unison. They were always doing that—singing a weird country song at a weird time. They were best friends and I was a third wheel, the new kid in town.

I wonder if I'll ever feel at home here. I kicked the log again.

Wondering. Mom says I'm always wondering about something. "Curious Anne," she calls me. Gee whiz! The biggest thing I'm wondering about now is why Mom and Dad decided to leave paradise and move to this old town. I mean, Mountain Center. Whoever heard of Mountain Center? You can tell why it's called that—a dumb old town stuck in the center of the Sierra Mountains. Excuuuuuuse me, Sierra Nevada, just like Mr. Millerton corrected me today in my twelfth day—yes, I'm counting—of eighth grade at—you guessed it—Mountain Center Middle School.

Anyway, there I was living in paradise.... In case you don't know where that is, it's right smack between Disneyland and the beach—like the Pacific Ocean, I mean. Anyway, it was just about perfect, with a mall in any direction, when my parents—Mark and Kate Shepard—decided they were bailing out.

I can sort of see their point. I mean, a riot, an earthquake, and a fire in one year would make anyone wonder if the whole place was going to warp away or something. But move to a town of five thousand people? You'd think the biggest town in the county would have more people than that!

I gave Maria and Alia my you-weird-person look.

They seemed so alike yet so different. Maria stands about five feet six with an athlete's build and almost-black eyes. Alia comes up to my nose and is lucky if she's a size one. Her round wire frames hide her gorgeous blue eyes and her thick blonde hair matches Maria's style exactly.

They each have their own unique look. Not like me. About everything on me is average. Average brown hair, average length. Average brown eyes. Average build, except that I'm already five feet eight and still outgrowing my jeans.

"Don't worry, Annie," said Maria, grabbing my arm. She was the outgoing one. She came right up to me on the first day of school and said, "Hey, who are you?" I couldn't believe it.

"You'll catch on. We know all the country songs. It's a game we play—to see if we can both come up with the right song at the same time."

Alia took my other arm. "Here, we'll walk you to your front door, madam. I think it's really neat that your mom and dad own the new feed store—what's it called?"

"Duh. Mountain Center Feed Store," I said.

"Duh," they chimed.

"Yeah," said Maria. "I love going there. They have mice and baby chicks...and free kittens."

"Free kittens," said Alia. "That reminds me. Have you guys heard about all the missing cats? Our cat, Stripes...."

"The striped one?" asked Maria.

"Duh," said Alia. "Yeah, the striped one. Anyway, he's been missing for five days. And Tyler...."

"The guy in math who wears glasses?" I asked.

"Yeah, him," said Alia. "Anyway, he said today one of their cats—a Siamese—she's gone too."

"Maybe they eloped," said Maria.

"Duh," Alia and I chimed. I was getting it.

"No," I said. "I think something weird is going on. My dad says someone else came in for a free kitten—said their cat was missing. And I hear cats all the time, but never see them."

We walked along in thought, slowly approaching my house. It's not hard to miss, since it's the only house at the end of a road that winds behind the fairgrounds and dead ends at the national forest. The house is "quaint," my mother says. It's definitely not L.A.—about 80 years old, two-and-a-half stories tall, with tall pointy rooflines and scalloped trim. My room is on the second floor with a little balcony thing that half a body could fit on—I say *could* because the door's nailed shut. I guess the last mother who lived there was paranoid.

We walked the eight steps to the front porch that went around three sides of the house and sat down on the porch swing.

"So why'd your folks move here?" asked Maria.

"They say they escaped," I said. "They used to be attorneys in L.A. They got tired of freeways and gangs. The earthquake was the last straw. Dad says they traded their briefcases for buckets."

"And hoes, it looks like," said Alia, pointing to my mom's garden, wrapped in fencing and netting.

"Yeah," I said. "In L.A. we had a swimming pool. Now

we have a garden. It was the first thing that Mom did when we got here in June—plant this garden. But there's not much left now, especially since some animal raided the thing before we got the netting up."

Alia nodded. "That'll happen when you live at the edge of a forest."

"But animals don't build fires," I said, pointing to where we had been. "And they don't make little sparkles of lights here and there, either."

"Little lights?" they chimed, leaning forward.

"Yeah, sometimes, when I wake up in the middle of the night, I'll see a light here or there on the fairgrounds. Once by the racetrack. Once by the horse arena. Once by the grassy area where the carnival goes."

"Now that's spooky," said Alia, shivering.

"I'd like to see that some night," said Maria.

"Hmmm," I said. "Maybe we could work that out."

"Yeah," said Maria. "And we could pretend we were, you know, sleuths."

"Like Nancy Drew," I said.

"Right," said Maria. "And solve this fire and lights mystery at the fairgrounds—and maybe some of the other weird things going on in this town. There are a lot of strange things going on in Mountain Center—did you know that, Annie?"

My eyes about popped out of my head. Strange things? Sounded kind of fun for a curious person like me—even in this dumb town.

"Well, if we're going to be sleuths, we need a name," I said.

Alia sighed. "My mom doesn't like me being out at night yet. I can only go to friends' houses after school."

I sighed. But then I had a thought. "That's OK, Alia. We'll just call ourselves the After School Sleuths."

Maria smiled. Alia smiled. "Cool," they said in sync.

Alia checked her watch. "Hey guys, I've gotta run. This sounds great. Let's get together again after school tomorrow and figure out our game plan." Both girls put on their backpacks.

"I'm sure glad I got to know you," I said.

Maria and Alia looked at each other and smiled. At the same instant they sang with a twang, "To know my gal is to love my gal...."

Then they burst out laughing. I just shook my head. Girls were definitely different in Mountain County. They put their arms around each other's shoulders and walked down the lane, spinning around in a circle, giggling and waving with their other hands.

I swung back and forth, back and forth, watching Maria and Alia walk back down the road. I was just about to lug my backpack into the house when...

"Aaaaaahhhhhhh!"

It was a woman's scream coming from the fairgrounds!

2

ON THE TRAIL

It took me about three seconds to think of the three things I could do. I could stand there and do nothing and wonder for the rest of my life what that woman was screaming about. Scratch that one.

Or I could run down the hill and scale the eight-foot fence and probably get my new jeans ripped on the barbed wire that goes all along the top. Scratch that one too.

I chose Door Number Three. Leaning against the house was my 18-speed mountain bike, fully equipped with mini-pack and water bottle. At least now in Mountain Center it made sense to have a mountain bike. The only mountains in my part of L.A. were the freeway on-ramps which weren't a good place to see if all your gears work.

I zipped down the hill, around the corner, and through the pedestrian entryway in the fence. One cool thing about

Mountain Center was that they left the fairgrounds open so people could walk through them or get their exercise going around the grandstand track. Not as cool, of course, as power walking around a three-story mall as Mom used to do in L.A., but....

Right ahead of me by the horse barns was the source of the screams. That was pretty easy to figure out, since she was still screaming.

"And stay out of here," she said, shaking her finger into empty space. "It's not nice to scare poor innocent ladies like me." She suddenly noticed that I had approached.

"And what do you want?" she demanded, putting her hands on her enormous hips that were covered with enormous Farmer-in-the-Dell-type overalls. Somehow that just seemed to match her short stature and curly short hair.

I screeched to a stop. "I, uh, just heard you screaming and wondered if you were okay."

"Teenagers!" she said. "They're always doing something they're not supposed to do. I was just checking out these stalls—to see if they all got cleaned out after the horse show last weekend—and when I opened this one, out popped these two boys. Those two boys!"

She pointed toward the north gate. As I spun my bike around I could see two figures zipping through that pedestrian entryway. One of them I recognized as Tyler.

"M'am, I...."

"Mabel," she interrupted. "M'name's Mabel Thornton. And you?"

"Annie," I said. "Annie Shepard. I live...."

"Oh, yes, Shepard," she interrupted again. "You live in the old house behind the fairgrounds."

"Yes, m'am, umm, Mabel," I said, "but how...."

"Not how, dear, who," she interrupted once more. "Who did you say you saw?"

"I think it was "Ty—"

"Tyler Hawkins," she finished for me. "Tyler Up-to-Somethin' Hawkins, I should say."

"Up to something?" I asked.

"Up to somethin'," she repeated. "That boy is always doing somethin' for no good. Pranks, I mean. Grease on the monkey bars in the kiddie park. Bubble bath in the fountain. Gotta keep an eye on that boy."

"Should I follow him, m'am?"

"Follow him? What for? And as though our conversation had ended, Mabel turned around and returned to her stall checking. "Stall 12. Clean. Check. Stall 13. Clean. Check. Stall 14...."

I shook my head as I watched Mabel walking away, talking to her clipboard. "What for?" I muttered to myself. "Why to see what he's up to and where he's going...and who he's with." I just didn't understand adults sometimes, especially these Mountain Center types.

I hurried toward the back gate. If Tyler and friend hung around the fairgrounds a lot, they might know something about the fire and lights. Or maybe they even were at the bottom of the whole thing. I stopped outside the gate and looked left, then right. There was no sign of them either way. But left was the long way into town and right was the short way. Right.

It didn't take long to find them. They were walking up to the window at the Frosty, about two blocks away. Now, the Frosty—a sky-blue building in the shape of a pyramid—is something Mountain Center has that L.A. didn't. L.A. had McDonald's, Burger King, Taco Bell—you name it. Everything except a Frosty. A frosty is swirly soft ice cream in a cone, but *the* Frosty has a lot more than that—from hamburgers to Indian Tacos.

I was thinking about how yummy an Indian Taco would taste when I realized that I had better zip behind the Frosty so the guys wouldn't see me. Why, I didn't know, but I figured I was on my first sleuthing lead, and I had better not blow it. So I cruised across the park-like lot next to the Frosty, across the mini-bridge that went over a mini-creek and around behind the Frosty. I parked my bike and crept around the far side of the building. Standing between two tall shrubs I could see them without being seen.

Tyler pushed up his brown eyeglasses and brushed aside his sand-colored hair as he leaned into the Order Here window. Then he tucked his plain blue T-shirt into his jeans. "We'd like two Pepto-Bismol milkshakes."

Jason tried to stifle a grin that wrinkled his freckled face and jiggled his curly red hair. "No way. You know I don't want a Pepto-bismol milkshake. M'am, I'd much prefer a milk of magnesia malt."

The lady inside the Order Here window was tapping her pencil on her order pad and pursing her lips. She pushed back the strand of hair that had fallen out of her French twist, straightened the top of her clean white apron, and breathed deeply. "We have chocolate and vanilla and half-and-half. We don't have Pepto-Bismol. And we don't have milk of whatever."

Bonnie—that's what her name tag said—was starting to close the window, but Jason leaned into it with a smile. "We'll have two medium half-and-halfs, please, m'am, and thank you for your patient and courteous service."

I was surprised that Bonnie filled the cones. In L.A. you could get shot for saying something like that to the wrong person. But a minute later she handed them through the Pick Up Here window. "Two half-and-halfs for two half wits!" she called out loudly enough for Tony to hear across the street at Tony's Auto Parts. Which wasn't necessary since Tyler and Jason were sitting underneath the Pick Up Here window, leaning against the building.

All of a sudden I realized that they were headed around my corner and so I hightailed it back behind the Frosty and crouched on the far side of a big tree that stood near the stream. There were several wooden picnic tables behind the Frosty in the grassy area and, rats! Jason and Tyler sat on the one farthest from me.

But it was close enough to catch a few important words.

"...cats...."

"Cats? ...cool...."

"...lost...fire...."

"...fire?"

"Yeah...fire!"

Lost cats? Fires? Tyler and Jason definitely knew something about some of the weird things that had been going on lately. I tried to lean closer around the tree to hear better.

"Hey, Jase," Tyler said, "look at that great bike over there. I wonder whose it is."

"I don't know. There's no one around. Maybe someone just forgot it."

"Yeah, maybe we should ride it back downtown and turn it into the sheriff's office."

"And give ourselves a ride home at the same time? You're always thinking, Ty."

It took me about three seconds to figure out the three things I could do. I could sit there and let the boys take my new mountain bike with water bottle and mini-pack. Scratch that one—Mom would kill me.

Or I could saunter out from behind the tree, say "Hi, guys, I'm new in town, and I was just eavesdropping on everything you just said." Scratch that one.

Again, it was Door Number Three. In less than one second I jumped over that mini-creek, onto my bike, and left Tyler and Jason standing in the dust. Or, I should say, sitting in the stream. I guess I scared the wits out of them, and they fell on the slippery grass and landed bottoms down in the water.

Boy, did I have a story to tell Maria and Alia!

3

FEED STORE FRICTION

About halfway between the Frosty and home was the feed store, so I stopped there. I had to admit it: I kind of liked my parents having a feed store instead of just commuting to an office every day. Although their hours working at the store were probably just as long as at the law firm, I did get to see more of them. And they're always glad to see me.

"Annie! Hi, sweetie! Boy, am I glad to see you. I've got a customer." Mom took off her work gloves and wiped her forehead with the back of her hand.

Mom—Kate Martoni Shepard—was not average. Her short, shiny brown hair bounced when she moved. In fact, just about everything with Mom was in constant motion. Her hands moved when she spoke, and her face spoke even when she wasn't talking. She looked pretty slim in her T-shirt and jeans. But I couldn't believe she had already traded her designer ones for Wranglers. Work gloves? I knew what was coming.

"Hi, Mom, I'm just on my way through...."

"You're just in time to clean the pens. Here, you can use these." She handed me her gloves.

I dragged the trash can down the aisle. Our feed store is like a mini-zoo. On the far wall is a whole row of pets—hamsters, puppies, rats, rabbits, mice, fish. They're fun to watch. But not fun to clean up. Every day the trays and pens have to be emptied and washed and freshened with clean shavings.

I always thought I wanted a zillion pets. But after a few times of cleaning their messes, I decided I'd just stick with one of Shakespeare's kittens. Shakespeare is Grandma Rose's cat. Grandma Rose Martoni is my mom's mom who lives right smack in the middle of Mountain Center. She used to be an English teacher and, you guessed it, she taught a lot of Shakespeare. She got Shakespeare last winter as a buddy for Chaucer, her older cat, and well, it turned out Shakespeare was a girl cat, not a boy. My Grandma Rose is pretty smart about books and stuff like that, but she's no scientist.

Anyway, Shakespeare is expecting a litter of kittens. When we knew we were moving to Mountain Center, Grandma Rose said one of the kittens could be mine, if Mom and Dad said it was okay. I want one with a lot of spunk. Grandma Rose wants me to call him Steinbeck, but I want to name him myself.

Phewwww! I pulled out the tray from underneath the rabbits. I've never understood how such cute little things can make such a stinky mess. And you have to watch out for Chester. If you get within marking distance, he'll get you. I hope they sell him soon. I'm tired of yellow stains on my tennis shoes.

A loud pounding interrupted my thoughts. "I'm just tired of people like you trying to run me out of business." A hunched-over, bony man with a pitted face was leaning into the checkout counter waving his finger at my mother.

"I'm sorry, Mr. Greely. We just thought we were doing a public service. People have unwanted litters all the time. Gee whiz, my own grandmother had a surprise litter. So we let people put them in our free kittens' box and usually they're gone within a day or so. It's good for business. They usually buy a bag of food and kitty litter and all the things a kitty needs. And we give them a brochure from the vet about spaying and neutering."

"That's exactly my point, Mrs. Shepard," Mr. Greely said. "You're only thinking of yourself. What about me? I'm trying to raise fine pets as a sideline. But with your giving them away, no one wants to pay money for a cat. You're killing my business, Mrs. Shepard."

"Well, I certainly didn't mean to, Mr. Greely. I'd be happy to keep some of your cats here at the store on consignment." Mom was pretty good at negotiating—something she learned at the firm, I guess.

But Mr. Greely began snorting and pawing his feet. I thought he might charge like a bull, so I sort of not entirely accidentally knocked over a bunch of buckets that was stacked in the middle of the aisle.

"What was that?" Mr. Greely shouted peering over his shoulder and down the aisle.

I cleared my throat. "Just me, Mom!" I shouted. "Just cleaning up here in the horse row! Everything's fine. Just doing a little rearranging."

Mr. Greely snorted again. "I didn't know anyone else was in the building."

"It's just my daughter Annie," Mom said. "Well, as I said, I'd be happy to work with you on this...."

"You don't seem to understand, Mrs. Shepard." Mr. Greely had lowered his voice. "I don't want to work with you. I've had a fine little business raising quality cats for our community. And it's going to stay that way. I'm going to see to it." Then he sort of gasped and held his chest. He seemed sick or something. He paused for a moment, thinking into space. Then all of a sudden his eyes focused on something I couldn't see and he smiled. It wasn't a nice smile. It was an I'll-get-you smile. And then he looked at my mom. "Free cats, huh? Good for business, huh? We'll just see if there are any more free cats around. We'll just see." And then he walked out.

"Whew!" Mom looked kind of white. "Glad he's gone. I don't care if he never buys another sack of cat food from us again. He's definitely a little nutso."

"Yeah, Mom," I said. "It's hard to believe that a man like that would be raising cats. Do you think he'd actually do something to hurt cats?"

"I don't know, Annie," she said. "It's hard to tell with people you don't know."

It didn't take me long to finish up the cleaning job. And since I was worn out and grimy after just forty-five minutes, I knew Mom would be wiped out after a long day at work—too wiped out to cook. It's hard work figuring out what to fix, put it all together, and clean it all up afterwards. So I did the only thing I could think of to make her life easier.

I suggested we get Indian tacos at the Frosty.

4

A SPARK OF INTEREST

By the time I had done my homework and chores at home, it was nearly dark. Upstairs in my room, I plopped myself, stomach down, on my beanbag chair right in front of my balcony door window. In my left hand I had Dad's binoculars. In my right hand I had Mom's portable phone. I wasn't going to miss anything—fire, lights, or whatever. And whatever I did see I was going to report immediately to Maria and Alia. I wanted them to know they could count on me to stay on top of our first case.

What I didn't count on, however, was Link. Link is short for Lincoln, my brother, who is not short, and who is a junior at Mountain Center High School.

"Hi, Squirt." His large frame hovered over me as I continued to stare out the door. He wasn't half bad looking for a brother. The girls melted over his curly dark hair and deep set, dark eyes. But I was not butter.

"I'm not a squirt. I'm five feet eight inches tall now, which is a half inch taller than Mom."

"O.K., Queen Kong, give me the phone."

"Excuse me?" I moved the phone underneath the bean-bag chair and sat on it.

"I want the phone."

"Excuse me?"

"I need the phone."

"So do I."

"But you're not using it. You're just sitting on it."

"But I will need it. And when I do need it, I'll need it right away."

"And until then, Queen Kong, I'll be using it." Link grabbed the beanbag chair and flipped it and me so that I was flat on my stomach again but this time on the hardwood floor. But I quickly grabbed Link's ankles as he was leaving. If he'd been clear, he would have fallen completely to the floor. But instead, he flopped onto my bed.

"Ah, thank you," he said, completely unperturbed, even though I was still hanging on to his ankles. "I'll just call Crystal from here." And he proceeded to dial. "Oh, hi, Crystal. See? Told ya I'd call exactly at 8 o'clock. Yeah. Uh huh. Uh huh." I could tell this was going to be an exciting conversation, so I let go and let Link slink down the hall.

I turned off the overhead light, plopped down on my bean-bag chair again and stared out the balcony door window.

It is amazing how dark the sky is over the mountains and how many more stars you can see than in the city. I squinted my eyes and, for a moment, thought I was seeing stars down the hill on the fairgrounds. But, no, it was the bobbing of a...a light! And it was coming closer!

I got out the binoculars and focused in on the light. But it kept bobbing around behind the grandstand. And then it stopped—just about where I had seen the campfire the night before. For what seemed to be a long time it appeared to be moving around in circles. And then it appeared—the fire. A small spark, then gradually bigger and bigger until it glowed under what seemed to be logs.

I couldn't stand it, just lying there staring. I had to see if there was a who with the light and figure out why the who was there. I walked down the upstairs hall toward the stairs. But then I hesitated for a moment. I wondered if I should call Maria or Alia. I peeked into Link's room. "Yeah. Uh huh. Uh huh. Me, too." Link was still on the phone with Crystal.

I tiptoed down the stairs, trying to think what I'd tell Mom and Dad if they saw me going out the front door. "Just had a hankering for a zucchini, Mom." Nah. "I have to try and identify star constellations for science." Nah. They knew I was taking life, not earth, science. Maybe I could tell the truth—that there was a campfire on the fairgrounds and I wanted to check it out. Nah. They'd report it or check it out themselves and spoil all my After School Sleuths fun.

I had to go alone. But I needed to get through the front door, which was the only one in that old house that didn't squeak. Somehow I made it down the stairs without the wooden steps giving me away. Mom and Dad were in the dining room to the right past the living room, going over book work.

Dad had been gone for part of the day picking up hay. He'd missed the big scene at the feed store with Albert Greely.

They looked kind of homey there sitting at the dining room table going over bills and stuff. Dad was wearing his red plaid flannel shirt with his sleeves rolled up. His sandy blonde hair was a little disheveled and longer than how he wore it at the firm. He pushed his wire frames back up his nose with his pencil. He looked up for a moment from his figures, then stared at Mom. He smiled real big at her and she smiled back and leaned over for a kiss.

I figured this was a good time to make my move out the door. I reached for the brass knob, turned it slowly, carefully, pulled the door open and started to step through the threshold when it happened. *Squeeeeeaaaakkkk.*

"Annie." It was Dad with his eyes square on me over Mom's shoulder. "Annie Shepard, where are you going? It's dark out."

I had to think fast. "I know, Dad, that's why I'm going out."

"You're going out because it's dark?"

I walked through the living room toward them. "Yes, Dad. Ummm, it's just that in L.A. it doesn't get this dark and so I'd like to really experience the darkness of Mountain Center...since it's so dark...uh, right now...outside." I brushed my hair back with my hand and smiled halfway up one side of my mouth. Ooops.

"Annie, you're brushing your hair."

"Right, Dad." I knew he had me.

"When you're trying to cover something, you brush

your hair like that with your hand."

"Aw, Dad, sometimes I wish you'd never been a defense attorney. It's just that I...." I hesitated. I so badly wanted to see the campfire up close and yet I couldn't give anything away yet. Not yet. "I think I'd better go to sleep or I'll never get up in the morning."

Dad smiled. "OK, Annie. Case dismissed. Good night, dear."

I trudged back up the stairs. It was tough being a sleuth when you couldn't even check out clues after dark. Good thing we decided to call ourselves the After School Sleuths. But the days were getting shorter. And I knew then that we'd have to do some slippery sleuthing. When I got in bed, I set the alarm for an hour earlier than usual—6 a.m. I'd get up at the crack of dawn and catch whoever it was that was behind those lights and fires.

5

A PHOTOGRAPH
HALF

I surprised everyone by getting up, dressed, and out the door by 6:15. I ran down the hill toward the back of the grandstand. Through the chain-link fence I could see it—the remains of a campfire just about twenty feet away. Small traces of burning embers were all that were left, though. No one was in sight. In fact, there didn't seem to be any clues around.

I was itching to look around more closely, so I ran the length of the fence around to the back pedestrian entrance, then back to the site. Like the day before, there just seemed to be the fire. I kicked at a partly burned log and then squinted. There was something smoldering off to the side—a piece of paper or something. I picked it up. It was a half-photo portrait of a woman. I could make out pretty clearly the left half of her from waist up—medium-length brown hair, brown eyes, a shy smile. She was holding a bouquet of flowers—like it was a wedding or something, except that she wasn't wearing white. She had a pale peach dress on.

My heart was pounding. Someone had put that photo in the fire. Why? You didn't tear up and throw someone's picture in the fire unless you were mad. Who would do that? A man, probably. The figure I had seen with the flashlight the night before? I had to find out who the woman was. If we—the After School Sleuths—could find out who she was, we'd have a strong lead on who was camping there. Maria and Alia would know—they knew everyone in Mountain Center.

I got to school about a half hour early, hoping Maria and Alia remembered that we were going to meet. They got there shortly after I did, strolling together arm in arm as though they hadn't disconnected from the day before. Petite Alia had on a denim jumper that went to her ankles with a T-shirt underneath. Taller Maria had one on too, but it was way above her knees. With their matching hairdos, they looked like wannabee twins. Kind of funny, and yet, I wished I were their triplet.

"Whatja find out?" they asked in unison.

I told them all about Mabel and chasing the boys and their conversation about "fire" and "cats." And I told them all about the binoculars and the campfire and trying to sneak out and finding the fire remains that morning. And the man in the pet store.

"Wow, you sure are taking this sleuth stuff serious," said Maria.

I smiled. "And not only that, I found something. Look!" I reached into my backpack, unfolded the napkin from my sack lunch I had wrapped the photo in and held it out.

Maria and Alia looked bug-eyed for a moment and dropped their mouths wide open.

"Did you..." Maria started.

"...find it in the fire?" Alia finished.

"Sure did. Do you have any idea who she is?" I asked. But both girls shook their heads. "It's kind of hard to make her out—with it just being half a picture."

"I have an idea!" Maria said, reaching for the photo. "I could reconstruct her."

"Huh?" I asked.

"You know, finish the picture. We've done that in art class— finish the other half of a cutout picture. I'm pretty good at it."

Alia nodded. "She is."

"I'll work on it during art class right before lunch. It'll give us something more to go on. We can show it around or something—see if someone else knows her." Maria carefully rewrapped the photo and pressed it in a pocket in a notebook from her backpack.

"You guys are great," I said. "We're going to work together real well. Only you could have figured that out, Maria."

Maria and Alia suddenly looked at each other and smiled. On their silent cue, they sang, "Only you...are the one who...would love me, too...." And off down the corridor they went, arm in arm. Leaving me in the hall dust again.

At noon I timidly looked across the lunchroom for Maria

and Alia. That ruined the Lunchroom Technique. When you're in junior high, there's a technique for finding a place to sit in the lunchroom when you're all alone. When you enter the room, you sort of begin to rummage through your lunch bag and casually bring something yummy slightly out of the bag—but enough so people would notice. You have to be careful not to make eye contact with anyone. If no one spots you or your yummy thing and asks you to sit down by the time you cross the room, you find an end seat and pretend you like sitting by yourself. That's a lie, of course, since no one in junior high wants to sit alone. But at least it saves embarrassment.

But this time my look didn't embarrass me.

"Annie!" Whew. It was Maria. "Annie, over here!

She had even saved a seat for me. "Look what I did!"

I stared at the completed portrait of the mystery lady. It was amazing. Maria had seemingly reconstructed the photo perfectly. Surely someone would recognize the woman. Below the picture on the cardboard mat she had neatly printed: "Guess who this is! If you can guess correctly, you will win a prize. Call A.S. at 555-1416."

"Omigosh!" I gasped. "You used my phone number and initials, Maria."

"Well, wasn't this your idea?" Maria rolled her eyes and pouted.

"Yes, but what if they...if someone finds out who A.S. is and tracks me down."

"Um, Annie," said Alia, "I don't mean to hurt your feelings or anything, but isn't this what we want—to find out who this person is? And who's behind the fires and all?"

I sighed. "True." It had all been my idea. Someone's phone number had to be listed. And, I figured, it might as well be mine. I smiled. At least they were including me in something, and at least I was even sitting with someone at lunch now. "Okay. So what are we going to do with it?"

Alia smiled back. "At the Cattails Cafe they display all kinds of local art—paintings, drawings, photographs. I bet they'd display this too. It's good enough and different enough."

"Great idea, Alia," said Maria. "Wow. Just imagine: My artwork up there with all the local greats."

"Cattails?" I said. "That reminds me. Has either of you heard anything more about any missing cats? I keep hearing them at night but never see them. Do you think these two cases could be connected?"

"The fire and the missing cats?" Alia said.

"Yeah," I said. The other two sort of nodded their heads in interest and started digging out their lunch goodies. I bit into my granola bar and hoped I wouldn't hear any more jokes about it being a dog biscuit from the feed store. Nope—just happy munching. Maybe I was getting somewhere.

6

A DITCH AND
FRUIT WHIRLIES

I met up with Maria and Alia after school. After all, we hadn't really made our game plan. I told them that my Grandma Rose's house was on the way to the Cattails Cafe and that we could stop there for a homemade cookie or two. I'd heard that a way to a friend's heart was through her stomach. They thought that was a pretty good idea, and so we started heading that way when we saw Tyler and Jason. Right ahead of us. And talking. Loudly.

"I don't really want to go to the fairgrounds again," said Jason. "We got yelled at last time."

"Aw, c'mon. It'll be fun. And while we're there we can check out the cats," said Tyler. "You chicken or something?"

"Nah. Okay, but just for a few minutes."

Maria looked at me, and I looked at Alia, and she looked at all of us. And we didn't have to say a word. We knew we had a lead on something. And the fairgrounds was a short-cut to the main part of town and Grandma Rose's any-way...so....

We followed them. I could tell by Maria's and Alia's actions that it was going to be hard to teach them the fine art of sleuthing. Maria darted to the side of a building, peeking out from behind until the boys were a ways ahead. Alia ran and hid right behind her. I mean, it was almost silly watching those two. They looked more suspicious trying not to be seen than if they'd just walked along the sidewalk like I was.

As we approached the fairgrounds, they ran out of cover and began to creep behind me.

"You guys are absolutely ridiculous," I whispered. "If they look back at us, they'll be sure to know we're following them."

And right on cue, as if they could have heard me, Tyler and Jason turned around. And stopped dead in their tracks. So I stopped dead in my tracks. And the silly two behind me bumped into me because they didn't have the sense to watch where they were going.

"You girls aren't following us, are you?" asked Tyler, hands on his hips.

"Umm, no, of course not," I said since I was the one in the front and the other two were beginning to giggle behind me. "We're going to my Grandma Rose's house—it's a shortcut this way."

"And do you always walk like that?" asked Jason. "In single file?"

The other two peeked from around me at that point. Maria looked at her fingernails and picked at an imaginary hangnail. "Um, no, it's just that it's hot out and Annie here...um, she offered to shade us, since she's tall and all and, I mean, why should we all be in the sun when she can shade us so nicely? After all, she is the new kid in town."

I felt my face turning red in a combination of anger and embarrassment, especially when the two boys began to laugh hysterically and hoot at me. They ran off toward the animal barns when I finally exploded.

"Shade you? Excuse me? Shade you? I am no one's shade, thank you very much."

"I'm sorry, Annie, I just..." Maria started.

"...she was just trying to get us off the hook," finished Alia.

"Yeah, honest," said Maria. "I mean, we are a team, right? The sleuths after school, at your service."

"Hey, we could make an acronym out of that," I said.

"An acronym?" asked Maria.

"An acronym is an abbreviation that spells a word." I paused, thinking. "How about S-A-S-S-Y? Sleuths After School Serving You. SASSY!"

"Cool," said Alia.

I looked down the road. "Hey, they're getting away. Let's catch up and follow them."

We ran after the guys, slipped through the west gate, and peeked around the first cattle barn. They, unfortunately, peeked around too, saw us, and took off. They ducked into the front door of the pig barn, ran down the middle aisle, and then out the back door. We were about a building away when we followed into the building. But they took off into the lamb barn. We figured we could follow them through the beef barn and then the range cattle pens and on and on, so we headed to Grandma Rose's.

Grandma Rose lives two blocks from the feed store. In fact, about anything in Mountain Center is two blocks from anything else. It's just that small a town. It only took us a few minutes before we were opening her wrought-iron gate and admiring her pink flowers. I'm not very good at flower names, but it seemed to me Grandma Rose had in her front yard about every pink flower that exists. I knew what was on the trellis against the house—roses. And framed inside the trellis was Grandma Rose, in, like usual, a rose-print duster.

She spotted us right away, put down her book and got up from her wicker chair. "Hi, girls!"

"Hi, Gram." We reached for each other as I climbed the stairs to her white clapboard, one-story home. "Gram, these are my friends, Maria and Alia. We're on our way downtown, but I thought you might...." I paused, smiling a little.

She smiled, too. "...like a fruit whirlie? And a cookie or two?" When I nodded, she motioned us inside. "Now, don't I know you, Alia?"

"Maybe from church, Mrs. ummm," Alia said.

"Grandma Rose," Grandma Rose corrected.

"Okay, Grandma Rose. I think it's neat how you live just two doors from Mountain Baptist Church. My family just started going there a couple months ago."

"Well, I don't know all the young folks like I used to. I used to teach English at the high school. I knew all the kids' names then. Oh, I'm so forgetful! *Forget*, hmmmmmm.

Aunt Rose's eyes focused far off as she began to recite:

Sweet Love of youth, forgive, if I forget thee,
While the world's tide is bearing me along;
Other desires and other hopes beset me,
Hopes which obscure, but cannot do thee wrong!

That's Charlotte Bronte. *Wuthering Heights*. Ah, such love. That Heathcliffe. Such foolishness too."

Maria and Alia looked kind of big-eyed. I bet they hadn't met anyone like Grandma Rose before. She was always quoting from some great literature...or even worse, the Bible. That was really embarrassing.

"I know," she said as she stuck strawberries, bananas, and ice into her blender, occasionally popping a strawberry into her mouth. "Here's a better one: 'Can a woman forget her sucking child, that she should not have compassion on the son of her womb? Yeah, they may forget, yet I will not forget thee.'" She smiled broadly. "That's God. In Isaiah of the Bible. Much better." She triumphantly clicked the on switch and watched her concoction whirl around.

Moments later she poured fruit whirlies before our eyes and pulled some health cookies out of her cookie jar. Now, her fruit whirlies have always been out of this world, but her health cookies are not exactly terrific. Grandma Rose is totally into healthy stuff—no white sugar anything in her house and fresh veggies out of her garden. So sometimes her cookies are not exactly what you'd expect. In fact, they kind of look like the horse cookies we carry in our store. Which is why I never carry any in *my* lunch to school.

We slurped up our fruit whirlies while Grandma Rose asked

about every question someone could ask about school, our teachers, what we're learning, what books we're reading. She had a way of looking and listening that made you know you were important to her. She sort of soaked you up in her eyes. Which was kind of nice.

"Gram, we've gotta go," I said, wiping my mouth. "It was great—the whirlies and stuff."

"Yeah," Maria and Alia said together.

"Well, thanks for stopping by," Grandma Rose said. "And in your travels far and yon, keep an eye out for Shakespeare, will you?"

Maria and Alia raised their eyebrows. I could see they knew Shakespeare—the real one—had been dead a very long time.

Grandma Rose laughed. "No, dears, I mean my *cat*, Shakespeare. She's been missing since last night."

"Missing?" Maria, Alia and I all gulped at once.

"Yes, and I don't understand it. She's going to be a mother soon and...."

"And I get to have one of her kittens," I finished. Could Shakespeare be the latest cat kidnap victim? "Are you, ummm, worried, Grandma Rose?"

"Well, I am a little concerned. It's just not like her. Plus I'm lonely with just old Chaucer here." She picked up the sleepy tabby from the front doormat.

My two partners got that smile in their eyes again and I could feel a country song coming on.

"Lonely, lonely, I'm the only...." They walked down the sidewalk, crooning.

I gave Grandma Rose a hug and let her eyes soak me up again. Glancing at Maria and Alia, I kind of knew how Grandma Rose felt. But I sighed. Together we were going to the Cattails Cafe. That was a start.

7

HEY AND HAY

Two blocks later we were at the cafe. A couple of high
school girls were sipping something at a corner table. The
only other person there was a waitress who was putting fresh
white tablecloths on the round tables and straightening
wildflowers in old Coke bottles. On the barn siding walls hung
all kinds of art—photographs of mountains and faces and
paintings of things you recognized and things you'd never
figure out.

We approached the waitress who was wearing jeans, a
tie-dyed T-shirt, and a plastic nametag that said "Princess."

"Hi, Princess," said Maria.

"Greetings, child of nature," said Princess, half bowing
toward us, with a spacey look in her eyes. "How's your karma
today?"

"Haven't checked it yet," said Maria. "But my gas and oil

41

are fine."

Princess laughed, holding her side. "You are so funny, brown-haired one."

"*Maria*," said Maria. "Anyway, I have a picture here. I wondered if you'd display it for me. It's a new kind of art. I call it Missing Person."

"Like wow," said Princess. "This is as glorious as the universe itself. I'm going to put it right here and put this one somewhere else." Princess took down one of the few paintings I understood and put Maria's picture in the center of the whole wall. "I just love this. Many of us are cut in half, you know, and looking for that missing other half."

Princess just stood there staring at the picture and we stood for a second staring at her. There were definitely some different kinds of folks in Mountain Center. I didn't necessarily think that was bad—it sort of made life interesting. People in L.A. were all different too—but different in a different kind of way. We said goodbye, but Princess was still staring, trancelike.

"I've got to get home," said Alia. "I have to get my homework done before teen night at the church."

"I don't know about you, Alia," said Maria, "going to church during the week. Is it fun?"

"Yeah," said Alia, "we do weird stuff. Tonight we're going to have a watermelon seed-spitting contest."

"Sounds like an expectorating experience," I said.

"Yeah," said Alia, "we expect a big crowd."

I figured I'd walk with Maria and Alia as far as the feed store. We talked about our case and decided that Jason and

Tyler probably had something to do with the fire, and that the crazy man at the feed store had something to do with the cats. We hadn't exactly figured out if they had something to do with each other. But we did agree to call the boys to see if they were home and check the fairgrounds again for more clues.

When we reached Mountain Center Feed Store, Maria and Alia decided to visit the mice and baby chicks. Link was behind the counter filling in for Mom who was talking with a salesman. The girls were really disappointed that there weren't any free kittens, and I wondered aloud about the man in the pet store and his threat. The missing cat thing was really beginning to give me the creeps.

A boy about Link's age stepped up to the checkout counter. He took off his Giants baseball cap and nervously combed his light brown hair back with his left hand. He shifted his weight from the left foot to the right, then back again. And then he tucked his cap into the back side of his jeans and rolled up the sleeves of his blue work shirt. He had a long, sad face. "Excuse me. I'd like to ask about the Help Wanted sign you have in the window."

"Sure. Uh, hi, uh, your name's Jeff, right?" Link was fumbling under the counter for something. The other guy nodded. Jeff pulled out a paper and set it on the counter. "Let's see...here's the application form and a pencil. Just fill this out. We haven't had anyone else apply yet. It's a job bucking hay and filling people's feed orders and a lot of lifting work like that. You interested?"

"Yeah, sure. I need the work." The boy Jeff picked up the

form.

"Just make sure we have a phone number so we can contact you." Link took off his Dodgers cap and smoothed back his hair.

The boy fingered the form. "I don't have one. If that's a problem, I could check back."

Link smiled. "Hey, that's okay. I could find you at school. Don't worry about it."

When Mom cornered me about cleaning the cages, Maria and Alia remembered that they had to get going home. Couldn't blame them. But we agreed to keep the lines open to pass news back and forth about two of our prime suspects: Tyler and Jason.

8

A CATTY PROBLEM

Mom was sure surprised when I said good night early and vanished to my room. Link was working on a history paper on his computer, so I had full custody of the phone. I still had the binoculars from the night before and opened the windows on either side of the balcony door.

Then I stood and looked at that door. What was the use of having a balcony if you couldn't open the door? And besides, it would be easier to keep a lookout on the balcony. So I decided to open the thing. I turned the knob: It wasn't locked. I poked my head out the left window. As I had thought, it was nailed shut. Three nails were driven into the woodwork—one near the top, one near the bottom, and one near the doorknob.

I looked around my room for something to pull out the nails. Dad's motto was: There's a tool for every job. And he certainly believed it: He had a kazillion of them in his shop. But Mom's motto was. Whatever works. I think she used everything but a hammer to hang our pictures when we moved to Mountain Center—a stapler, a rolling pin, a bird figurine made out of marble.

I grabbed my curling iron off my dresser. Leaning out the window, I could just reach the bottom nail. It was bent over, so I caught it in the curling iron and twisted it back and forth until it came out. The middle one was easier to reach and came out easily. The top one, though, was just out of reach. Then I realized that if I could reach the nails, I could probably pull myself onto the balcony. I pulled myself outside onto the windowsill, then inched toward the balcony, holding onto the upper window. I swung my left leg onto the balcony railing, then let go with my left hand, then right, reaching for the railing and shifting all of my weight.

At that very moment I realized why the door had been nailed shut. The railing swayed left, then pulled off the balcony. I reached for the doorknob and my weight on the door broke the last nail loose and I swung it open, plunging back into my room.

After a deep breath I surveyed the damage. The railing swayed with just a finger touch. It was rotting from weather abuse. In fact, the whole balcony was a rotten mess. If I had stepped onto the balcony, I might have fallen through to the front porch!

I shut the door quickly. I didn't want Mom and Dad to see what I'd done if they'd heard the noise. But I didn't hear any steps. They probably thought it was just me bouncing off my mini-trampoline again.

And then I looked at myself. My T-shirt was ripped—probably got stuck on a nail. And a small gash on my right arm was bleeding. "Ow!" Delayed reaction. I reached for a Kleenex.

"Ow!" Was that an echo? I leaned out the window.

"Ow!" I said again.

"Meeoowww!" No, that wasn't an echo. It was cats! Lots of them were whining, coming from the direction of the fairgrounds. I looked through the binoculars toward the campfire area. But all I could see was black. No campfire that night. But there definitely were several cats crying—one after another. And then all of a sudden the noise stopped. I waited in the quiet for a light or a voice or something. But everything was perfectly still, except for the occasional swish-swish of the sprinklers wetting the grass at the grandstand.

Maybe I should call Maria or Alia, I thought.

I looked at my hands. I'd written Maria's number on my left hand and Alia's number on my right hand. Or was it the other way around? I couldn't remember. I figured whosever number it was, I'd know the voice.

"Hello."

"Ummm, Alia?"

"This is Maria."

"Maria, this is Annie. I...."

"Let me call you right back. I'm on another line." Click.

So then I figured I'd call Alia. At least I knew which was her number. Maybe she wouldn't be too busy to talk to me.

"Hello."

"Umm, Alia? This is Annie. I...."

"Gee, Annie, I'm on the other line. Let me call you right back." Click.

I sighed. They were talking to each other. Oh, well. There in the pitch black of my room I waited, with the binoculars in my left hand, phone in my right. I grabbed one of my dozen pillows from my bed, opened the balcony door and laid the pillow right on the threshold. I stared and listened toward the fairgrounds, but there was nothing but black. No more cat noises and no fires. But it was unusually warm. I turned over, looking up toward the sky. Cloud bunches appeared overhead and then just seemed to hang there like cotton candy. And then....

Ring! I clicked the phone on. "Hello?"

"Hi, Annie, this is Maria. No luck. The guys were both home. I called Tyler and Alia called Jason."

I turned onto my tummy again. "Yeah," I said. "There was nothing much here." I paused for effect. "Except *cat* noises."

"Cat noises?"

"Cat noises. Coming from the fairgrounds. There seemed to be several of them—no, more than several—maybe a half dozen—all at once. And then the sounds completely disappeared. It was weird. First you heard them. Then you didn't."

"Did you see anyone?"

I told Maria I didn't see anyone, although I could have scared them away by falling through the balcony, climbing the tree to the roof, and then sliding down the drainpipe. Okay, so I didn't fall through the balcony. Or climb the tree. Or slide. I may have exaggerated that a little bit, but I didn't want Maria to think I was a wimp after not being let out of the house the other night.

Later I kind of felt bad about my story, so I did what Grandma Rose would have done. I prayed.

Hello? God? Are you there? I'm, uh, not sure you know me, but I'm Annie.

I looked around the room, waiting for something. But there wasn't a sound. Dumb. I mean, what did I expect? Quadrasound?

God, I'm just going to figure you're there. Somewhere. Wherever that is. Anyway, I'm down here in Mountain Center trying to make a friend or two. But you knew that, didn't you? Well, gee whiz, God, it's tough.

I paused a moment, breathing deeply and counting to two and a half. *I'm sorry about stretching the balcony story somewhat. okay, a lot. But how do you impress someone in this old town?*

But as I was watching those cotton candy clouds, there was just a bunch of quiet from the other end. And I fell asleep, right there on the floor.

The next morning I awoke to cat noises again, so I called Alia and asked her to call Maria and meet me at the back gate as soon as they could. I threw on the closest pair of jeans and a T-shirt from the cleanest pile on the floor and raced downstairs. Mom was making French toast and bacon, and I took two of each and a napkin, stuffed them into my backpack and barreled out the front door over her "Dear, you shouldn't eat on the run like that."

Maria and Alia were running from the other direction when I reached the employees' back gate. "This way," I pointed and headed toward the grandstand. It would just take a couple of minutes to race past the horse arena and bleachers to the grandstand. Surely the cats were those that were missing. And hopefully they would still be there, and we could rescue and return them to their rightful owners.

In just a few seconds we were across the track and at the edge of the grass in front of the grandstand. But just as we started across the grass a voice came over the loudspeaker: "Stop! No students allowed during school time. Turn around now and get where you should be—on your way to school!"

We could vaguely make out the outline of a man in the announcer's booth at the top of the grandstand. And then he appeared—a tall man in brown coveralls. He looked like the man I saw on the tractor lawn mower. He didn't yell or anything, but did take off his cap and pretended to shoo us away.

"Bummer," said Alia. "We were so close."

"Well, I don't hear any cat noises, Annie." Maria shifted her backpack and glared at me.

"Do you think I'd make that up?" I tried to swallow the lump in my throat.

"Well, I've noticed sometimes a new kid in school will do something weird to get attention," said Maria. "Is that what you did, Annie, make this whole thing up?"

Alia stepped between us. "Maria, that's not fair. Remember the photo? And the missing cats? There do seem to be some weird things happening. We're just not there at night to see and hear what Annie's seeing and hearing."

That gave me an idea. I breathed in deeply. "Why don't you two both spend the night? I...I could check with my mom at lunch and ask her for sure. Then you could see for yourselves. And maybe, if you're with me, Mom and Dad would let us take a walk on the fairgrounds tonight."

Maria and Alia both smiled real big. I knew I'd hit on a good idea. If the cats were part of the mystery, we would find out that night.

9

GHOST STORIES

Mom thought the idea was cool, so Maria and Alia came in time for dinner. I was glad that Dad decided to barbecue that night. The brick barbecue in our backyard was one of the things that Dad liked right away about our house. It was a big home-made thing at the back edge of our brick patio. On the back side you could barbecue stuff. On the front side was a big round pit in the middle of the patio, perfect for your own little campfires at night. I knew Maria and Alia would love roasted marshmallows over that campfire.

Grandma Rose even came for dinner. We sat around the campfire roasting shish kebabs. Maria and Alia—and every-one else actually—thought that was pretty neat: meat and vegetables stuck on willow sticks from our backyard. But I knew that Mom was just trying to get rid of her cherry tomatoes and three kinds of squash. Pretty sneaky.

Grandma Rose was in rare form, dressed in rose-floral short pants—she called them pedal pushers—and a matching blouse. She loves being invited over to our backyard. She says it's like a retreat—the soft grass surrounded by huge pine trees filled with little furry animals. Mom liked it too, until the little furry animals started raiding her garden. But the netting took care of that.

I could tell Grandma Rose was searching her brain files for something while she was poking her veggies on her stick. And sure enough, after a few moments she turned around to the group and said:

"Then a sentimental passion of a vegetable fashion
  must excite your languid spleen,
An attachment a la Plato for a bashful young potato,
  or a not too French French bean!"

"We don't have beans, Gram," I said. "We picked them all. Is that it, Gram?"

She poked on the last cherry tomato with a flourish. "For now, dear. That was Gilbert from *H.M.S. Pinafore*—one of my favorite musicals."

Maria and Alia shook their heads back and forth in exactly the same movement. At first I thought they thought Grandma Rose was a little touched in the head. But when they stuck their veggies on the same way and sat on either side of her at the fire, I figured differently.

It was fun toasting the dinner that way and then pulling it all off into a sandwich roll of barbecue sauce and gobbling it down. It got dark pretty quickly and Mom got out the marsh-mallows. But there are only so many ways you can roast and eat a marshmallow before you're sure your teeth are going to fall out of your head from pure grunge weight.

And we were all staring quiet-like into the fire, poking it with our sticks when Grandma Rose had the best idea. "Let's tell ghost stories."

Link rolled his eyes. "Gram, we're not, you know, kids anymore. I haven't done that since Cub Scouts."

"Well, Lincoln," Grandma Rose said, "you might not be a kid anymore, but I still am. And I'll start."

I got up from the fire circle and inched my way backward to peer around the side of the house to check the fair-grounds. Nope, there weren't any fires yet. Or cat sounds that I could make out.

Mom walked over to me, carrying serving bowls. "Anne Rose Shepard," she said, "you have company. Now go be polite and listen while your dad and I do the dishes."

As I returned to the fire I could see Maria and Alia had totally forgotten that we had a mission that night and were absolutely wrapped up in Grandma Rose's story.

"...and then the mistress of the house went crazy after her children died. And people say she built passages that went nowhere. And doors that wouldn't open. Or other doors that opened into walls." Grandma Rose stood up, fully into the drama she had created, and walked around the fire pit. "But at night people said she could be seen walking through those same doors and disappearing into nowhere."

Maria and Alia's eyes were bugging out and just about ready to drop into the fire.

"And?" asked Maria, pulling her jeans jacket around

her and zipping it up. "And then what happened to her?"

"No one knows," said Grandma Rose, stopping and staring into the fire. "She disappeared. Some say she is still alive in that old mansion. And others...and others say...she's writing those new Nancy Drew books and making big bucks off eighth grade girls like you!"

"Oh, Gram!" I said.

"Mrs. uh, Grandma Rose," said Alia, "you are a great storyteller."

"It comes from practice," said Grandma Rose. "When I was teaching English at Mountain Center High School, I heard some of the wildest stories."

"Yeah?" asked Maria.

"That's right," said Grandma Rose. "Every time an essay was due in my class, I could count on a good eight or ten wild stories from my students on why they couldn't get it done the night before."

Link chuckled. "I know what you mean, Gram. In fact, I've told a few myself. But I've got a good ghost story. Ya'all want to hear it?"

I rolled my eyes. Link somehow had picked up a country accent from working in the feed store and listening to country radio.

"Sure," said Maria, nodding with Alia.

"This is a true story," said Link. "At least that's what the locals say. Anyway, north of Mountain Center off the highway a ways there's a religious cult. A bunch of them sort of living in a commune thing."

Grandma Rose nodded knowingly.

"And people say that they're known to do weird things with their ceremonial fires...like even sacrifices!"

"Sacrifices!" said Maria and Alia together.

"Sacrifices. Lizards, rodents...even cats. They...."

"Link," I interrupted.

He ignored me. "...they...."

"Ahem, Link!" I kicked his right boot which was pushing a log in the fire and that made the log fall and sparks flew everywhere.

"What's your problem?" He started to kick me back but Grandma Rose stood up.

"Lincoln. Anne. Stop, please. Link, Annie is not so diplomatically trying to get you to change the subject. You see, Shakespeare has been missing."

"Well, gee, Gram, I didn't...." But all of a sudden he stopped. And cocked his head as if listening. And then we listened too.

It was the meowing again. Coming from the fairgrounds.

"There it is again!" I said. "There are cats on the fairgrounds. Someone has cats on the fairgrounds!"

"Do you think...maybe Shakespeare is there?" said Grandma Rose.

"Well, let's go find out!" I said. "We'll run to the back gate. Link, can you go over the fence somewhere?"

"I'll give it a try, m'am," Link said, bowing.

"We'll meet you there," I said. "Come on, Maria, Alia. Let's go! If there's really a cult and there really are cats missing, maybe they're there...and...and maybe Shakespeare and Stripes are with them!"

10

ANOTHER CAMPFIRE CLUE

It took us awhile to get to the closest gate. It was a cooler and moonless night so we had to inch along the fence to find our way. I led, with Maria stepping on my heels and Alia stepping on Maria's. We finally found the gate, only to discover it closed. There was a sign on it that we squinted to read aloud together when a car drove by: "Employee Entrance Only. Hours: 7 A.M. to 7 P.M."

"Bummer," said Maria.

"Now what?" said Alia.

"Hopefully Link is already there," I said. "Let's go on to the pedestrian entrance."

"Gee," said Alia. "I wouldn't think they'd have horses out at this time of night."

I shook my head. "Alia, that's *equestrian*. Pedestrian is someone on foot."

"Well, horses have feet," said Alia.

"It's weird how the big gate is closed and the other one is always open," said Maria.

"I guess they trust people on the fairgrounds," I said, feeling my way along the back fence. "But they don't trust people in cars."

"That makes sense," said Alia. "Teenagers could hot-rod around the place and mess up the grass and things."

We squeezed through the wide steel poles at the entrance and found our way to the edge of the wide lawn where the carnival always was set up. There was one wet problem: The wide-sweeping sprinklers were on. And not only that, because it was so dark, we couldn't tell which way they were coming or going.

"Now what?" asked Alia.

"I guess we get wet," said Maria.

We listened for a few moments to try and figure out what the sprinklers' pattern was. Tick, tick, tick, tick, *whoosh*. Tick, tick, tick, tick, *whoosh*. Tick, tick, tick, tick, *whoosh*.

"Now!" I yelled. "Follow me!"

Somehow I made it past the one sweeping to my left, then past the one sweeping to my right. But then, Splash! Right head on, I got it full-force from one I didn't figure on in front of me. Again, Maria and Alia, used me like a football lineman, and I blasted my way through, the other two wimps crouching behind me.

At the other side, I stood dripping wet. My Dodger blue-hooded sweatshirt hung past my knees. My jeans were about to fall off my hips. And my tennies were weeping. I couldn't really see Maria and Alia too well, but they sure weren't squish-squishing like I was when I walked.

"Hey, we made it!" said Maria.

"Yeah, that wasn't too bad," said Alia. "I just got one swipe on my backside. How about you, Annie?"

"Does this answer your question?" I squeezed out my sweatshirt and ten gallons of water hit the pavement. "Next time, you guys are the human shield."

"Well, we're almost to the grandstand," said Maria. "We just have to go past the chapel, the little schoolhouse, and the gazebo."

"Gee," said Alia, "I didn't know they had any wild animals here. Do you think it's safe walking through here at night?"

"Alia," said Maria, "the only wild animals we're going to meet tonight are the weirdos messing with those cats we heard."

"That's scary enough," Alia said. "I'm not sure I want to go ahead with this."

"Well, if you want to stay here, we'll see you later." Maria started heading toward the big shadow before us that I had also guessed was the grandstand. I hung back a little. I didn't want to leave Alia alone, but I didn't want to miss out on any new discovery either.

"Come on, Alia," I said. "As my dad says, what's the worst thing that could happen?"

"We could get hit over the head, sacrifice-barbecued over the fire, and then become someone's cat food for the next month."

I gulped. I hadn't thought of that. "Well, I suppose there's a very minor and yet very distinct possibility of that happening, Alia," I said. "But get real—in Mountain Center?"

"You're right, Annie," said Alia. "Let's go."

Somehow I had convinced Alia. But I myself wasn't convinced. Why would someone be stealing cats in a town like this? Why would they be hiding them at the fairgrounds? Why were these fires and lights coming and going? Something weird was waiting up ahead for us, and I wasn't sure I was ready to meet it head on.

Whoever or whatever it was, it certainly was getting advance notice that we were on our way. My tennies were still squish-squishing. Maria was shushing me, as if I could really do anything about my squeaky tennies except take them off. Which I wasn't about to do. And Alia was praying. Loudly.

"Oh, Lord, protect us from the cat *bugles* ahead. We are weak, yet You are strong. You are our Protector and our Shield. Amen."

I think she got the shield idea from me. I had decided I liked Alia. She had a weird vocabulary, but she had a kindness about her—kind of like Grandma Rose's. She certainly prayed like her anyway. And I didn't mind that, either. It sort of calmed me down, even though by then I felt like a popsicle—a drippy one.

Ker-Thunk! Ker-Thunk! Ker-Thunk! One by one we passed through the turnstiles to the grandstand area. To the right were the stairs. Ahead was the rear of the grandstand.

"Well, we can go ahead and meet them face-to-face or we can sort of surprise them from the top," I said.

"I think we should climb to the top," said Maria. "That way we can stay hidden better. What do you think, Alia?"

"I think that if we climb to the top, it'd be a long way to fall after they hit us over the head."

Maria groaned. "Alia, no one is going to hit us over the head."

"No?"

"No," Maria and I said together.

"Let's just go straight for the campfire," I said. "I see a glow coming from around the bend of the back of the grandstand."

"You're right," said Maria. "Let's go!"

It was going to be all right. I was sure of it. Besides, Alia was reciting the Lord's prayer. Maria and I led the way, arm in arm, feeling our way around the back side of the grandstand. Alia was behind us, holding on to the soggy hem of my Dodger blue sweatshirt.

There wasn't a sound by now, except for my tennies squish-squishing and Alia praying. "...and forgive us our..." Ahead of us we could clearly see the campfire glowing. "...and lead us not..." Closer, closer we tiptoed looking all around for figures of something, someone. Listening for the cat sounds we clearly had heard earlier. And then we were there, right at the campfire, huddled together, still peering around, still listening. But there was nothing, again! No one. Nothing. Except....

"Look, guys," I said. "Someone's been here." I pointed to two large opened cans of beans bubbling in the middle of three small logs.

"Two someones," said Maria, reaching to the ground.

She held up two spoons that had been resting on a tree stump near the fire.

"I don't like this," said Alia. "Those someones could be watching us right now."

I nodded. But for some reason I just didn't want to leave. Two cans of beans. Two spoons. That didn't seem to be much evidence for all our daring. And still there wasn't a shred of anything to tie all this with the cat noises. I felt around the campfire area.

"What are you looking for, Annie?" asked Maria, who also dropped to her knees, feeling around.

"I don't know," I said. "It just seems like there would have to be something more here."

"Eeewwwww! Ahhh! Oh, gross!" I jumped.

"What is it, Annie?" asked Alia, coming to my side.

"Some kind of dead animal," I said. "It's something with long fur."

"Where?" said Maria.

"Here." I felt around, found a stick, and then used it to lift the thing into the light of the fire. It was....

"Cat fur?" Maria asked.

"Ooo, yuck," said Alia.

I picked it off the stick. It was a large wad of grayish cat fur—like it had been yanked out or the remnants of....

"Do you think someone was..." started Maria.

"...oooo, yuck, frying cat here tonight?" finished Alia.

"Yes, fellow sleuths, someone strange has been doing something strange with what was probably a cat," I said, looking around eerily.

Alia looked around, too. "B-b-by the way, wh-wh-where is Link?"

"I d-d-don't know," I said.

"C'mon, Maria, let's get out of here," said Alia.

Maria grabbed Alia by the arm and took off back down the grandstand wall, through the turnstiles, and lickety-split through the sprinklers. I followed them. And this time, somehow, we went so fast that none of us got wet—or wetter, I should say. And I hung on to the wad of cat fur that surely was a sign that someone weird was doing something weird with cats on those mysterious fairgrounds.

11

COINCIDENTAL GUESTS?

Fright can sure motivate a person. When Mom described the whole process behind "root canal," I started brushing my teeth twice a day. When Mrs. Pearson, my English teacher, mentioned "detention," I got caught up on my vocabulary overnight. And that wad of cat hair motivated the three of us to break the in-the-dark, half-mile record. We couldn't believe, however, what we saw waiting for us on the front porch.

Sitting on the porch swing was Link, all calm, cool, and collected. He wasn't the surprise, though. Swinging their legs over the porch railing were Tyler and Jason.

"What?" Maria said, poking Alia and me. "Do you see...."

"Oh my goodness," said Alia, "the cat *bugles*."

"It's *burglars*, Alia," I said. "We don't know for sure, but this certainly is a coincidence."

Link noticed us first. "Hey, where have you been, wet head?"

I'd almost forgotten that I looked worse than a wet hamster. "The question, Link, is where *you* have been. Umm, we had a certain place we were going to meet—did you forget?"

Link leaned back and started swinging slightly. "Well, I was on my way down the hill and then ran into Tyler and Jason."

I turned to Tyler and Jason. "And what were you guys doing on the fairgrounds at night? And what are you doing here now?"

Tyler cleared his throat. "There's a simple explanation for that, Annie."

"Yeah, real simple," said Jason. "Go on, you tell her."

"Well, I was until you.... Anyway, Jase and I have a game we play—dodge the sprinklers. On moonless nights like this we try to run from one end of the grassy area to the other without getting wet."

"Yeah," said Jason, "the guy who gets the wettest has to buy the other guy a milkshake at the Frosty."

"Looks like you lost, Jason," said Maria. "You're almost as wet as Annie here."

"Yeah, I just didn't have the old timing down tonight," said Jason.

I scratched my head. The sprinkler deal didn't sound too far-fetched to me. "OK, I believe the sprinkler story, but what were you doing on this end of the fairgrounds? And what are you doing now?"

"We were about to try one more round of sprinkler running when we saw a glow from behind your house. So we decided to go check things out."

"Yeah," said Jason, "we thought it might be a forest fire. That happens a lot this time of year, you know."

"We were coming around the front of the grandstand when we ran into Link." Tyler's right eye was twitching. He rubbed it.

"So you never found anything on the fairgrounds?" I asked.

"No—uh, nothing. Why would we?"

"Oh, nothing," said Maria. "And you never heard anything? Or saw anyone?"

Tyler and Jason looked at each other, shrugged, and shook their heads. They had definitely been up to something more than sprinkler dodging. Their shoes, for one thing, were covered with mud. And there wasn't any mud in the grassy areas and walkways. They had been somewhere else on those fairgrounds. And they knew something more.

"Hi, guys." Dad appeared at the front screen door. "Annie, would your friends like to roast a couple of marshmallows with us in the backyard?"

Tyler stood up. "Well, gee, thanks, but we've got to get home."

"Yeah," said Jason, "it's getting kind of late. My folks are probably sending out the posse."

"Yeah," said Tyler, "my dad's probably home from Oregon by now. He's bringing home a new cat."

"Hey, that's right," said Jason. "Let's get going. Thanks, uh, Mr. uh...."

"Shepard," Dad said. "No problem, guys. See you some other time. Annie, you need to come in and say goodbye to your grandmother. She's still upset, you know, about her missing cat."

Cat? Cat? I looked at Maria and Alia. Their mouths were wide open and for the first time since I'd met them, it was obvious they couldn't think of something to say. And I thought if my eyes bugged out any more at that moment, they might fall out and bounce off the porch.

Tyler's dad was bringing home a new cat? I felt the wad of cat fur in my soppy Dodger blue sweatshirt. This just had to be more than a fireside coincidence.

12

CULTIC CONNECTION

Grandma Rose was disappointed, naturally, when I told her we hadn't found Shakespeare. But her cheeks rosied up when I told her we were on a strong trail of cat evidence and that she shouldn't lose hope.

She smiled and said:

"Hope springs eternal in the human breast;
Man never Is, but always to be blest."

"Shakespeare?" I asked.

She sighed. "No, honey. Alexander Pope. But here's another one: 'When God is in your heart, there's always hope within your grasp.'"

I knew this one. "Let me guess—the Bible?"

Her face all crinkled up and she reached over and gave

me a squeeze, which was a little embarrassing with Maria and Alia standing there gawking. "Gotcha, again, Anne dear. That one was a Grandma Rose original."

"Oh Gram!" I walked her to the door where Dad was waiting to take her home.

"Do we still have a date, young lady, for our once-a-month lunch tomorrow?"

"Oh, that's right!" I said. "I'll be at the store in the morning—can I meet you there?"

Grandma Rose nodded, blew kisses to Maria and Alia and headed out the door. Before I could even turn around, Maria and Alia were turning me around and grabbing me by the elbows.

"We have got to talk, girl," said Maria, pulling me upstairs.

"Yes," said Alia, pushing from behind, "someone's got to put a stop to those cat *bugles*."

"*Burglars*," I corrected. "OK, c'mon—my room's just up around this way."

Once in my room, we pulled the dozen pillows off my bed and they flounced on the floor.

"Cool room, Annie," said Alia.

"You obviously like blue," said Maria.

I smiled. She was right. My comforter was blue. My curtains and throw rug were blue. My dozen pillows were all in blue prints. I figured blue matched my mood here in Mountain Center.

I pulled the now-damp wad of cat hair out of my sweatshirt pocket. We all gaped at it. It half-filled the palm of my hand. It was striped in light and dark grays and was about an inch long. There wasn't any skin with it. It was as though someone had yanked it out.

"It's Stripes!" gasped Alia.

"You sure?" said Maria.

"I don't know," said Alia. "Maybe."

Maria and Alia continued to look it over while I changed out of my wet clothes into my warm blue sweats.

"Blue again?" asked Maria.

"Sorry! I just like everything blue—blue clothes, blue room, umm, blue...."

"...blue, blue, 'cause of you, and my dog died too" sang Maria and Alia, in sync.

I had had it. "Why do you guys sing those country songs?" I asked. "Nobody in L.A. does."

"It's about the only thing we can get on the radio here in the mountains," said Alia.

"Yup, good old K-O-R-N," said Maria in a tenor voice, "number one hundred on your dial with the best of country in the country."

After they got over their laughing fit—notice I didn't say "we" got over "our" laughing fit—we agreed we needed to do some brainstorming as Mrs. Pearson had taught us. I got down a couple of my horse posters, and we used the back side. I wrote Tyler's name in the middle and drew a circle around it. Then we tried to think of as many things about him as we could think of and wrote those things in other circles that came off spokes from the middle.

As Maria and Alia spoke, I wrote down the ideas: Hates

history. New cat. Does pranks. Best friend is Jason. Hangs out at fairgrounds. Dad's a logger. Mom works at courthouse. Younger brother.

"We're not coming up with much," said Alia, yawning.

"Let's do Jason," said Maria.

So I wrote down Jason's name in the middle and things associated with him. Hates history. Does pranks. Best friend is Tyler. Hangs out at fairgrounds.

"Fellow sleuths, this sounds familiar," I said. "Do some thinking here, huh? You have lived here a lot longer than I have. You've got to know something about these guys."

Maria and Alia closed their eyes for a few minutes. I thought Alia was nodding off, but then she said, "I think his father is a teacher or something."

"No, that's his mother," said Maria. "She teaches at Mountain Center Junior College outside town. Biology or animal science—something like that. His dad is older. He's retired, I think."

"No, he has a business of some kind," said Alia. "I know. Do you have a phone book, Annie? I could look it up."

"Yeah, his last name is Greely," said Maria. "Jason Greely."

I think I turned white because I felt like my stomach had hit the floor then risen up to my tonsils. "Greely?" I said weakly. "Greely?"

"Yes, Annie, Greely," said Maria. "What's the matter?"

"Don't you remember me telling you about the man in the feed store who talked about the stray cats—he was a real spooky guy?" Maria and Alia nodded in silence. "His name was Albert *Greely*!"

Alia stood up and started jumping around the room. "Ohmygoodness. Ohmygoodness. Ohmygoodness. "Whatarewegonnado? Whatarewegonnado? Whatarewegonnado?"

Maria stood up. I think she wanted to slap Alia back to her senses. But instead she calmly put her hand on top of Alia's head and made her sit down again. "There was an ad in the paper today about their business—Greely Pet something."

"I'll see if Dad still has it," I said. Fortunately, I grabbed it just as Dad was about to use it for fire starter. Mom and Dad still weren't used to the cold nights. I ran back upstairs and handed it to Maria.

She fished through the pages. "Here it is. Look."

I took the paper. I read the ad to the others:

Greely Pet Board and Care
We care for your pets while you care for yourself
Leave your loved canines and cats with us
Tranquilizing available
All types of obedience training offered

"Oooooo," I said. "Tranquilizing and all types of obedience training? He didn't exactly seem like the gentle type to me. Choke chains? Muzzles? Gas?"

"According to this ad, their place is just past the college on the outside of town," said Maria. "There's a number listed."

"Is it 555-2312?" asked Alia. "That's the number I called

for Jason."

"Yes," I said. "It's the same number. They must live right there."

"We could try the guys and see if they're home," Maria said.

"Just a minute, Maria," I said. "I think this news story is even more important. Sit down and listen to this." I folded the newspaper to the right story. "'Cops Find Animal Remains.'"

"Animal remains?" cried Alia.

I continued reading. "'Mountain County authorities are investigating cat remains found at a remote campfire Thursday. Sheriff's deputies who responded to a complaint from an anonymous citizen reported there was evidence that the site could be the hub of cultic activity. Deputy Sheriff John Smithee said the citizen was concerned that cats might have been used in a sacrificial ceremony. He cautioned local residents not to panic, but to take care about their pets' whereabouts.' And it goes on about how to take care of your cat."

"I've heard that there are a couple of weird cults around here," said Alia.

"Exactly what is a cult?" asked Maria.

"It's a religious group that distorts Christianity," said Alia. "It changes who Jesus Christ said He was."

"How could you change who Jesus was?" I asked. "I mean, I don't know much about church and stuff, but isn't it right there in the Bible?"

Alia smiled. "That's right. Anyway, cults can be a little weird or a lot weird—either way they're wrong. But it sounds like this cult is really scary. Cat sacrifices? That gives me the woolies."

"Willies," I corrected. "Maybe Link's ghost story was right."

"Maybe," Maria and Alia said, scooting closer together.

We finally settled down. I pulled out my trundle bed and Maria slept in one direction and Alia slept in the other direction. They were really impressed with my room—especially the balcony. Alia just about stepped onto it, but I saved her just in time. I had to remember to tell Dad about the thing—someone could get hurt out there some day. We told a few more ghost stories—as though we weren't scared enough by everything that had happened that night. And we agreed to check out leads at the feed store and the Cattails Cafe on Saturday.

13

NEWLY'S NEWS

We sleuths became sloths the next morning. We hardly even moved until nine o'clock, then dressed, ate cold French toast, and dashed out the front door in twenty minutes. I was supposed to help at the feed store by 9:30 A.M. while Link picked up a load of hay.

I grabbed my mini-pack, and Maria, Alia, and I ran down to the fairgrounds fence. It seemed completely peaceful—not at all like the night before. Ladies were strutting around the track. And the groundsman was checking sprinklers in the grassy area in the middle of the track. We parted ways at the feed store and promised to meet at the Cattails Cafe at one o'clock to find out if anyone had inquired about the picture.

When I got at the store, Mom was in the middle of a sale. Dad was out of town on business. So Mom mouthed one word as she smiled at me: "Feed." I didn't mind feeding. I just had to make sure I got the right feed to the right animals. There were about a dozen tubs underneath the cages with all kinds of animal feed. I was always curious what would happen if rabbits got hamster feed and hamsters got cat feed and cats got rabbit feed and.... I asked Mom once and she said, "Don't even think about it, Miss Curious."

I was still wondering about this when Mom asked me to dust. Wonder? I stopped to think. *Wasn't there a song Maria and Alia sang about wondering?* Oh, well, I wasn't sure I wanted to remember those songs. And I wasn't sure I would ever really be their friend or fit in at all with anyone in Mountain Center. I mean, how do you make friends with someone who has been best friends with someone else since preschool? It seemed impossible, and it seemed like I was always going to be a third foot...or was that wheel?

You cannot believe the dust that can collect on stuff in a feed store. The big door in the back is always open and I think we could keep somebody working full-time just dusting the shelves. I started with the horse stuff. I've always liked horses and hoped I could get one when we moved to Mountain Center. Dad said that when the weather got colder, the prices on horses would start going down, so maybe by Christmas I could get one. But he said I'd have to earn the hours at the store to pay for half of everything—the horse, the feed, the tack.

I was fingering a really pretty headstall with a horsehair design when I heard:

"Kind of big for a cat, Annie." I turned around. It was Alia, grinning. And Maria was with her.

"Hi, what are you doing here?" I put the headstall back on the wall hook.

"Mom said I could look for a new blanket for my horse for winter. My old one's falling apart. Maria's helping. She's had her horse longer than I have. Do you have any winter blankets?"

I dropped my dustrag. "Sure, over here. We have these three and can order any of these pictured here." But as I pointed out the wall poster, Maria and Alia ducked behind the display and dragged me down with them. "What are you...."

"Sshhhhhh," said Maria. "That's her."

I looked toward the front door. A woman wearing a long, multi-colored gauze skirt and pink flipflops had entered. Wrinkles—happy ones—lined her clear, peachy-colored face. Her greying brown hair, which I guessed went down to her hips, was swirled like a frosty cone on top of her head. She was looking at the cat items against the wall. She picked up a can of something, looked at it for a moment, then put it down and walked to the back counter.

"That's who?" I whispered, peeking around the horse blanket display.

"People say she's a part of that cult mentioned in the paper." Maria peered at her over my shoulder.

"The cat sacrifice one?"

"That's the one. My brother delivers her newspaper. She lives at the edge of town. He says there are cats all over her place—on the porch, on the fences, on the windowsills inside looking out. He says she probably has fifty or more cats."

I put my finger to my mouth. "Shhhhh. Listen."

Mom was making a sale. "More cat food? I thought you were already here this week."

The woman reached into her drawstring satchel attached to her waist. "Yes, I bet I'm one of your best customers, Mrs. Shepard. I have so many cats now I have run out of names. I started using the planets' names—Mercury, Venus, you know. Then I started naming them after moons and stars. Now I just can't think of any more names in the universe to use."

My mom cleared her throat. "It's, umm, nice for you to take in all these creatures, Mrs. ummm...."

"It's Newly. Just Newly. Thank you. It's just that I think we're all on this planet to be caretakers of some kind. We're all endangered species, you know. And I believe it's my cosmic call to care for cats."

Mom raised her eyebrows and looked toward the barn area. "Link! Link!" She paused, waiting for an answer, grinning nervously at Newly. "Oh, gee, that's right. Link is rounding up some hay. Umm, Annie, are you here? Annie?"

I jumped out from behind the blankets. Maria and Alia stayed hidden. "Y-y-yes, Mom?" I walked slowly toward the back counter.

"Come help me load some cat food, dear. Is your car near the barn, Newly?"

Newly stared at me as though she were looking into me or through me. I looked away and then at Mom, raising my hands in a question.

"Newly?" Mom asked again.

Newly shook her head. "Oh, excuse me. I sometimes nod

off like that. I must be getting old."

Old? I thought. *Newly doesn't seem old like Grandma Rose and her friends. She is just spaced—as though she is in some other part of the universe than we are.* I tried to smile politely, but I've never been very good at polite when I don't really feel like it. I just wanted Newly to leave. She gave me the woolies, I mean willies.

It turned out Newly didn't even have a car. She had a bicycle. She said she didn't believe in using carbon-whatevers that would shrink the earth's resources. So we loaded her fifty-pound bag of cat food in a cart that was attached to the back of her three-wheeled bicycle. She climbed onto the thing and headed off down the road, the cart wobbling back and forth, back and forth behind her.

Maria and Alia peered out the back door of the store. "Is she gone?"

I nodded. "That woman is a little strange."

"Just like her daughter," Maria said.

I turned around and looked at Maria. "Daughter?"

"Her daughter," said Alia. "You've met her. At the cafe. Her daughter is Princess—the waitress at the Cattails Cafe."

"That figures," I said. "Princess—just Princess. Newly—just Newly. It's weird, though. She keeps acquiring cats. Other people keep losing theirs. The police are finding animal—maybe cat remains, maybe cat sacrifices. Do you think there's a connection?"

"Could be," said Alia. "And this whole thing is making me into a big scaredycat."

"I know what you mean," I said. "My mom calls me

Curious Anne. I know I talk a lot, but I'm certainly not Courageous Anne. If we got messed up with those cult people, we might end up being a sacrifice ourselves."

Alia's face turned as white as our albino rabbit—as though she'd gotten too big a whiff of animal doo-doo. Maria sat her down on a sack of shavings.

"Hey," I said, "it's okay. We'll leave this cat thing alone for a while. And check out that mystery picture at the cafe instead. I mean, how dangerous could life be in a small town like this?"

Alia half-smiled at Maria. Maria half-smiled at me. I half-smiled at them both. We'd find out soon.

14

BROCCOLI SOUP
AND FAITH

That was about the longest morning of my life, dusting shelves and thinking about all the weird things taking place. I had always thought the city was a dangerous place, but then it seemed that even life in a small town could be scary. I'd always liked scary stuff like roller coasters and bungee jumping. But this evil kind of scary stuff was burning a pit in my stomach.

"Annie, dear." Grandma Rose stood in the doorway. *Right on schedule again*, I thought as I heard the twelve o'clock fire department siren go off. I grabbed my mini-pack and gave her a hug.

Grandma Rose was predictable in another way too: her wardrobe. Her as-always-pink-colored dress had roses the size of a dinner plate on it in the most awkward places. But her hat was great—a big floppy straw thing with real roses from her garden. It was amazing, the local people said, that we hadn't had our fall frost yet. I thought that was weird because I couldn't remember the last time we even had frost in L.A.

"Ready to go, dear? I'm famished!"

"Sure am. Let's go."

As we slipped into her brown and white '57 Chevy in the parking lot, Link drove up alongside her side of the car in the flatbed hay truck.

"Hi, Gram! Off to lunch?" Link hung outside his window.

"Yes, Lincoln dear. Would you like to join us?"

I grimaced. Lunches out with Grandma Rose were special.

Link noticed my face and returned the look. "Nah, it's okay, Gram. Jeff and I have to unload this hay. But I'll take a Fat Burger to go."

Grandma Rose winked and started inching out of the parking space. All of a sudden I felt a little guilty for leaving. Several customers had pulled up, and I knew Mom would be swamped in the store. One man walking toward the hay barn area appeared to be the groundsman from the fairgrounds. A mother and little girl holding onto her dress hem seemed disappointed when they saw there were no free kittens in the front cage. No one had come by recently with free ones—that was another weird thing happening.

I shook the thought away as we drove off. I was going to enjoy the lunch with Grandma Rose. We approached the Cattails Cafe in a couple of minutes. People still parked at a slant in the downtown area—just like in the old-time movies—and we got a spot right in front of the restaurant. There was even a free table on the outside patio, so we sat there.

A pony-tailed high school girl brought us menus and waited for our order.

I put my hand on Grandma Rose's menu. "Let me guess, Gram. Broccoli soup."

"Well Anne dear, I'm going to look at everything they have here, but you're probably right. I'm real partial to their broccoli soup. I don't make much soup anymore—it's too much work for just one person—so it's a real treat."

"Well, not for me. I think I'll have a...."

"...Fat Burger?" Grandma Rose finished. "I've noticed you're a creature of habit just like your grandmother."

I closed the menu. "Okay, you've got me. A Fat Burger and fries. And *no*, I won't have a milkshake this time. I'll have a...an orange soda. So there."

"Pretty venturesome, Miss Anne Shepard. I'll stick to my iced spiced tea. And one Fat Burger and fries later to go."

We handed over the menus and turned to listen to the music filtering out from inside the cafe. It was a fiddler that day— mountain music kind of stuff. The restaurant had a small platform in one corner where local musicians could perform for experience, mostly. They weren't really paid—usually they'd put out a hat or an open guitar case for donations. We listened for quite awhile without saying anything.

"I love that stringed music," Grandma Rose said, pausing to wipe at her cheek. "It reminds me of your grandfather."

"Grandpa Geno?" I asked. "I loved to hear him play. How

did he learn?"

Grandma Rose smiled. "His father taught him. Just like his father before and his father before. It was a tradition. And the fiddle got passed down from generation to generation."

"And does Uncle Bill play?"

The waitress brought our drinks, and Grandma Rose took a sip and patted her mouth with her napkin. "Yes, dear, a little. He didn't take it very seriously when he was younger, but now that your grandfather is gone, Bill is getting it out more often."

I took a sip of my soda. "And fiddling with it?"

"Right-o, Anne!" Grandma Rose said with a laugh. "Your Grandpa Geno, The Tease Supreme, would be proud of you!" She stirred her iced tea thoughtfully.

I stared at her. Her always warm brown eyes grew heavier. Grandma Rose had always seemed sort of eternal to me—someone who would always be there with her flower garden and fruit whirlies. But at this moment, she seemed older and sadder.

"You miss him, don't you, Gram?"

She reached for my hand and caressed it lightly. "Some days I do feel kind of lonely, dear."

I sniffed. "I know what you mean, Gram. Well, I'm sorry. No. It's not the same, is it?"

She looked at me. "It's been hard, hasn't it, Anne? Moving here away from your friends and the home you always knew?" I nodded. "Are you making new friends? Kids are friendly in a small town—seems that way to me, anyway."

The waitress brought our food and I reached for the ketchup and poured a large pile on my plate. "Yeah, they're friendly, all right. But making friends, Gram, is another thing. They've lived here forever. I'm new. I don't know that Joe Blow is Susie Q's cousin. I don't know what dumb thing Mr. Science Teacher did last year. It's stuff like that. I don't have a history with them. I'm going to be the new kid here for the rest of my life—even ten or twenty years from now!"

I picked up a French fry and swirled it in the ketchup. Grandma Rose stirred. "You do have a history here, Anne. The Martonis have lived here a long time—since the Gold Rush brought your grandpa's grandpa here and he opened his mercantile in what is now the downtown."

"I know, Gram. But nobody else knows that. I'm a Shepard, not a Martoni." I bit into my Fat Burger.

She sipped her soup. "Well, I understand. Even though I've lived here all my life, I feel alone sometimes." She sipped again. "But then I remember that I have a heavenly Father who is always there for me."

"Oh, right, Gram. Like you can reach out and touch Him."

She grinned. "Well, maybe not like the telephone. But we do talk. I pray, and I know He is listening."

"How?"

"Because He answers my prayers. You're an answer to my prayers."

"Me?"

"Yes, you, dear. I've been praying for an opportunity to

get to know you better, to see you more often. And here you are living in Mountain Center, and we're having lunch right now together."

I coughed. "So you're the reason I'm stuck here in this middle-of-nowhere place?"

Grandma Rose smiled. "I guess so, dear. The Lord and I, anyway. I think...no...I *know* He wants to get to know you better, Anne—and your family. And that's why all of you are here."

I took a sip of my soda. "And...and if I wanted to get to know Him...or whatever...what would that involve?"

"Just a prayer, Anne. He knows you're hurting. Tell Him you need Him. Ask Him to come into your life. And He will. He is the One True Friend, Anne, and He will never let you down." She paused and gave me that between the eyes look again. "I could pray with you right...."

I looked around. There were people sitting at the other three tables and others walking by. In fact, Maria and Alia were approaching and had just noticed us. And the waitress was coming over with the check.

"I don't think so, Gram. I've got to, to think about all this stuff a little. My friends are.... It's kind of...you know? Hi, Maria! Hi, Alia!"

"Hi, Annie," they both said in perfect timing.

"Hi, Grandma Rose," said Alia. "Are we interrupting something important here?"

I wiped my mouth with my napkin. "We're about done. Are you going to check on the picture?"

"Yes," said Maria, "we'll do that. You finish your lunch.

We'll come right back."

I stuffed the rest of my Fat Burger in my mouth and gulped it down with my soda. Grandma Rose excused herself to pay the bill. In what seemed like seconds Maria and Alia ran back out on the patio with pale faces.

"It's gone!" Maria said.

"Stolen!" Alia said.

"What?" I stood up. "Who...what...how did...." And then I had a thought. "Wait a minute. Princess works here. She is Newly's daughter. And all of a sudden cats are missing. And cats are showing up at her place. And now our picture is gone. Princess would have had the perfect opportunity to take the picture. Who would notice?" I scratched my head. "All of this has to connect somehow."

Maria and Alia stood there with blank looks on their faces.

"Well, one thing is for sure," I said. "Someone didn't want that picture up there in public. We just need to find out who that person is and why."

15

SLEUTHING AROUND

Grandma Rose understood when I told her I needed to take care of some business with Maria and Alia. She said she would let Mom know where I was when she took Link his Fat Burger and fries. I gave her a hug—right out in front of the whole world. I decided then that if I had to live in a small town, it was great living in the same one as Grandma Rose. It wasn't that she did stuff for me—but just knowing she was there when I felt alone. And it was kind of interesting the way she talked about God—like He was a friend and all. But then I had two friends, right there with me. So I figured God could wait awhile.

"We've got to talk to Princess," I said.

"Ohmygoodness. Ohmygood...." Alia started.

"Quit!" yelled Maria.

"Okay. Okay. O...." Alia paused, smiling a little. "...kay.

But let me get this straight. You want to go to her house? Out on the highway? The place with fifty cats? The future sacrificial victims?"

"YES!" Maria and I said together.

"It'll be great," I said. "And we can check to see if Shakespeare and Stripes are there."

Maria's eyes bugged out. "Wow! That's a great idea. 'Cause if Shakespeare is there, we'll know they're up to something. There's no way Shakespeare could have wandered that far from home. Right?"

"Right!" Alia and I said together.

It seemed like we were finally on the same wave length.

I thought so at first, anyway. But the whole half hour it took walking to the edge of town Maria and Alia spent jabbering back and forth about all the dumb stuff they did in the seventh grade. A science field trip to the Explora-something in San Francisco. A history camp-out near a gold mine. Like I wanted to hear all about who stuffed whose sleeping bag with tortilla chips! I was glad when we got to Newly's house.

"Look!" said Maria, tiptoeing behind a big bush. "There it is!"

I stared at the house. It sure wasn't what I expected. I thought a house with fifty cats would be gargantuan. Instead, it was a small house, probably not much bigger than my entire bedroom. The siding looked like it came from an old barn. And the two small windows and oval-shaped door made the front look like a face...watching us.

Someone driving by would hardly notice the place,

which was surrounded by shrubbery. Except for one fact. The entire house seemed to be covered with cats. They were on the paintless, rickety picket fence. They were on the porch and windowsills. A few were even on the flattish roof, decked out and obviously enjoying the mellow autumn sun.

"Think anyone's home?" I asked.

"You're actually going to go up to the door?" asked Alia, grabbing onto Maria's sweatshirt sleeve.

"Gee, I think so," said Maria, "and we might even knock. I don't think they'd bite us."

Alia chewed on her lip. "I don't know. Those cats might, though."

I started walking slowly along the sidewalk in front of the house. No one seemed to be around. I scrutinized the cat crowd. For as many as there were, they all seemed to look alike— a lot of tabby-colored or greyish, striped ones—ordinary kinds of house cats.

"Looking for Shakespeare?" Maria asked, coming alongside me.

I nodded.

"How exactly would you tell her apart from all the rest?" she said. "Didn't you say she was a gray cat?"

"It's easy," I said. "She looks like Shakespeare."

"Like Shakespeare?"

"She's got a little black goatee." I peered over the gate. "Shakespeare! Here, kitty kitty. Shakespeare!" That was the wrong thing to do. Just about every cat in the place came trotting up to the gate. And instantly they were rubbing up against my arms and legs and begging to be petted.

"I don't see Stripes," said Alia. "But they are kind of cute," she said, picking up a skinny black one. "I really do love.... Oh, no, look! A car is slowing down." She put the cat down. "Oh, no, it's stopping!"

"Don't look now," I said. "It's Albert Greely!"

Maria gasped. "As in Albert Greely, the cat breeder?"

He stopped his beat-up, beige pickup truck just ten feet from where we were standing at the front gate.

I gulped and nodded.

Alia gasped. "As in Albert Greely, the cat breeder who told your mom he was going to see to it that there wouldn't be any free cats around town anymore?"

He opened the door, stepped out, and slammed it behind him. He took a sweeping look at the cats all over the house and cursed.

I gulped and nodded again. I could tell Alia was going to freak on us again, so I stepped on her toe. Hard. My debate team coach told me once that if you pinch yourself or something when you're really nervous, you focus on the pain and forget you're nervous.

It didn't work.

"Oh, no! Oh, no! Oh, no!" Alia dropped the cat and started rubbing her hands on her jeans.

I decided not to pinch Alia again in a time of distress. Because Albert Greely turned and noticed us for the first time.

"You girls live here?" he grouched, moving closer.

"N-n-no, sir," I said, backing into Maria and Alia a little who were again hiding behind me.

"Then what are you doing here?" He took another step toward us, so that he was now within arm's length.

"W-w-we just like cats," I said. "W-w-we're just looking at the cats."

"Shhhhhhhe's right," said Maria, peeking out from behind me. "W-w-we just like cats. See?" She stroked one on the picket fence.

Albert Greely stood at the fence and looked again over the cat crowd. "I like cats too. In fact, I raise cats. And I'm always on the lookout for ones with interesting coloring. My customers like cats that are a bit unusual—you know, a cat that stands out from the crowd." He snorted. "But these cats look kind of ordinary to me. Guess I'm not interested."

And just as quickly as he had come onto the scene, he stormed off to his car, started it, and pulled away back down the road.

"Whew!" said Maria. "I thought we were dead meat!"

"Yeah," said Alia, "cat food!"

I laughed. "You guys crack me up. You're brave one moment and chicken livers the next." I laughed again and turned around to set down the cat I was holding.

And then my own liver jumped up to my throat. Because standing on the porch glaring back was Princess!

16

CAT CRISIS

"I bet it was one of you!" Princess hollered. She dabbed a tissue under her eyes. "You were the ones who did it!"

Maria, Alia and I looked at each other. What was she talking about?

"The picture?" I asked.

She stepped off the porch and walked the few steps to the gate. "Picture?" She shook her head. "What are you talking about?"

"The picture at the cafe," said Maria. "Remember? We brought in the picture of the woman."

"I wasn't talking about that," Princess said. "I was talking about our cat. When we got home this morning, there was a dead cat right in front of our gate on the sidewalk. Someone hit it with their car, moved it, and left. There wasn't a note or anything. Just poor little Pluto, left for a burial. Mother is beside herself. And is that why you're here—to apologize?"

I cleared my voice. "No, Princess. I'm sorry, but we don't know anything about the accident. And we're sure sorry about what happened." I looked around and gestured toward the other cats. "But you have so many other cats. Surely one will take its place?"

Princess's face exploded in a new torrent of tears. "Pluto was one of our first nine cats. He was one of the original great-great-great-really-great-grandfather cats. A natural death we would have understood. But to die because of the careless violence of this society." She stared into space for a moment.

Alia stepped through the gate, put her arm around Princess and patted her gently, looking at Maria and me. "So you don't believe in violence toward animals?"

Princess took a deep breath and blew her nose. "No. All of God's creatures are special. Gee whiz! We don't even eat fish sticks!"

I looked at Maria and Alia and all of us raised our eyebrows in understanding. This was obviously not a compound for sacrificial cats—not at least on Newly's and Princess's efforts.

All of a sudden, Princess looked at us quizzically. "Umm, exactly why are you three here? You said something about a picture?"

Maria stepped forward. "Princess, you remember hanging up the picture I drew?"

Princess nodded.

"Well, it's gone," said Maria. "We checked there today. Someone has taken it down. Do you know anything about it?"

"I'm sorry that I don't," said Princess. "It was still there when I finished my shift yesterday. I didn't work today. What a travesty—to steal someone's work of art. Theft, mutilation of animals—what is this planet coming to?" She sighed. "Well, special ones, I need to go console Mother. You understand, don't you?"

I couldn't stand it anymore. It was a perfect opportunity. I heard Dad say once that you have to ask the question to find out the answer. Sounded like lawyer logic at the time, but as I stood there looking at Princess it made sense. I had to know for sure. "Umm, one last thing, Princess. Do you...ummm...know anything about this cult—you know, the one in the paper? Someone said you and Newly might be members."

Princess turned sheet white, fell a step backward, then flushed red, and stepped toward me. I had an immediate sense that I'd said the wrong thing. She peered at me. "The one that performs animal sacrifices? How dare you make such an accusation. What a horrible thing to say or even think, for that matter! Mother and I love these little creatures. We could never....we wouldn't... I refuse to continue talking to you! Goodbye!" And she turned abruptly, ran up the walkway and steps and slammed the porch door behind her.

Maria crossed her arms and shook her head at me. "Wowee. Smooth move there, Sherlock. Real delicate approach. That really got us somewhere with this nice person who did us a favor the other day. I don't know about you, Annie. I think this whole sleuth thing has made you a little nutso." She started down the street.

"I just felt like I had to know for sure," I said, shrugging my shoulders and following her.

Alia walked between Maria and me. "It does seem as though we can cross Princess and Newly off our list."

I picked a leaf off a bush as I walked. "Maybe. They don't kill cats, and I can't think of a reason why they'd steal them—there are certainly enough of them around their own place."

"And they wouldn't have a reason to be wandering the fairgrounds at night," Maria said. "Let's sit down and figure this out." She pointed to a grassy lot sprinkled with flowers and park benches that served as a neighborhood park.

We reasoned that we still had the cult, even without Newly and Princess. If it sacrificed cats, its members would have a reason to prowl the streets at night doing weird things to find cats.

We also still had Tyler and Jason. We knew they wandered the fairgrounds at dark hours. And they had talked about cats on more than one occasion.

The last on our list was Albert Greely. He had a motive. He wanted to rid Mountain Center of free cats so someone who wanted a pet would have to buy his. If he were desperate, he might look for cats at night.

We agreed that we had to check out Albert Greely's place. We knew he had just been roaming around looking for cats, so we decided then was as good a time as any to take a peek into his operation. And it was just a few minutes' walk past Newly's house.

"And if he c-c-catches us there," asked Alia, biting her nails, "what will we tell him?"

"I know," I said. "I can tell him my mom and dad have promised me a cat—which they have. And that I am interested in seeing what cats he has—which I am."

"Great!" said Maria. "Maybe you won't say something dumb this time."

I sighed as we walked along. Or I should say, *followed* along, since Maria and Alia were arm-in-arm again and I was trying to keep my foot out of my mouth behind them. It didn't seem right. I was just being myself. Why couldn't they accept me as just plain Annie? I liked them the way they were. Or I would, I guess, if they liked me. I wasn't sure at that point which was harder to figure out—what the cats and fire mystery was or how to make a friend in Mountain Center. I hoped I'd find out soon.

17

PET BORED

It only took a hop, skip, and jump to get to Greely Pet Board and Care. Maria and Alia were hopping and skipping. I was jumping—from one conversation topic to another.

After boys, clothes, and television shows, we ended up on horses. Maria and Alia have horses. Alia's is her own. Maria's is actually her grandmother's that she uses. Mine, of course, is just in my head—sort of a mix of Black Beauty and Sham, the king of the wind. But because my horse is just in my head—even though it's real to me—I was on the outs in conversation again.

We did talk a little about music. I'm sort of a pop person. They like alternative—they alternate from week to week on what they like. One week they like hard rock, one week they like rap, one week they like pop. I figured that was sort of like the wildflower I'd just picked from the side of the road.

They like me. They like me not. They like me. They....

Whew! I was relieved when we made it to Greely's Pet Board and Care. But as we surveyed the grounds, it didn't look like a very mysterious place. A light blue ranch home sat in the center of the football field-sized lot. Ponderosa pine trees as tall as some L.A. skyscrapers randomly bordered the property. A blue metal building with "Greely's Pet Board and Care" painted on the roof was perpendicular to the house on the left. A couple of chain-link outdoor runs were attached to the building. Dogs and cats were in smaller runs on the other side of the house. Well-manicured lawn filled in between all of the facilities.

"No one seems home," said Maria, stepping up to the white picket fence. "But look." She pointed to a sign attached to the fence:

Cats For Sale
Inquire Within

"Well, we knew that," I said. "We just have to find out if Shakespeare and Stripes are among those they have here."

Alia coughed. "And h-h-how do we do that?"

"That's easy," I said. "Remember Plan A? I tell him my parents said I could have a cat, and I'm interested in seeing what he has."

"Right," said Alia. "I knew that." She nodded her head. "And...and what was Plan B?"

"We don't have a Plan B," said Maria.

"Right," said Alia. "I knew that. But...."

"Oh, c'mon, Alia," said Maria.

I opened the front gate and walked to the front door. Maria followed behind, dragging Alia by a loop in her jeans. But before I could even push the doorbell, the door opened. It was Jason himself.

"We don't want any," he said, his hands folded over his chest and grinning.

"We're not selling anything," I said. "In fact, I'm interested in buy...interested in your cats. Can we look at what you have for sale?"

Jason led us along a sidewalk to the left of the blue building and held open the door. "Welcome to our cattery." Inside was what looked like another house—but all for cats. We wiped our feet before walking onto the spotless off-white linoleum floor. Jason pushed open a screen door to the first room along the narrow hallway.

"These are our Siamese," he said.

Several litters of kittens played with their mothers and each other. They looked like little critters from a mystery, with their black masks and markings. Several romped over roller toys while others wrestled or climbed cat trees.

"These shorter haired cats are high strung," Jason said, teasing one with a length of yarn. "They like to play."

He then led us into the next room. "And these are our Persians. They're more of a grandma's cat—a lap cat."

The room looked almost exactly like the other one, except that those cats had long hair and smashed-in looking faces. Some were black, some were reddish, some were white.

"I think I've seen this one on a cat food commercial," said

Maria.

"Everyone says that," said Jason.

"These are all mamas and babies," I said. "Where are the males?"

"We keep them in cages in another room. They can get in fights, and we have to time the breeding just right. We also have some new litters in another room. You can see them if you'd like, but they won't be ready to leave their mothers for a while."

I peered down the hallway. "These are all purebred cats, aren't they?" He nodded. "And expensive?" I asked. He nodded again. I sighed. "But don't you have just your ordinary pet kind of cat?"

"Oh, we might have a few from time to time. Sometimes Dad will find a stray. Or sometimes someone will board a cat with us and never come back for it. Can you believe that?" He shook his head. "We normally keep those over in the board and care area. But right now we don't have any."

I could feel my foot reaching up again. "Umm, I bet your dad enjoys this. It must be fun working with animals all day."

"Yeah," said Jason, brushing back his curly red hair, "he does. Or he did, anyway. When Mom got the job at the college, he retired from his state job. He'd always had an interest in animals, so he started this business. He's put a lot of money in it. I think lately he's been frustrated that things haven't gone better. He and Mom argue about money a lot. It's hard having your own business in a small town. You'll find that out." He kicked at an imaginary pebble.

I thought about Mom and Dad spending long evenings—and sometimes hotly discussing things—around the dining room table over pages of figures and catalogs. I knew they had made a chunk of money from selling our house in L.A. And I knew they had been saving for a long time before we moved. But I also had overheard something about "give it a year." If the feed store didn't make it in a year....

"They'll find what out?" We jumped. It was Albert Greely standing at the back door of the house. He took off his rumpled canvas hat and pushed back his thinning gray hair. Before, in the feed store and at Newly's, he only seemed like an angry man. Here his eyes looked sad...and tired.

Jason walked over to his father. "Oh, nothing, Dad. They're just interested in cats. Did you get your medication in town? You should be taking better care of yourself, Dad. You want to give the doctor a better report next week." Albert Greely leaned on the doorknob. Both of them turned to go into the house.

"Oh, excuse me," said Jason. "Was there anything else you were interested in?"

I tried to ignore it—my curiosity streak that was itching me all over. It had gotten me in trouble at the last stop. And I didn't want it to get the best of me here. But all of a sudden I couldn't stand it anymore and blurted out: "Well, it's just that my grandma's cat, Shakespeare—grey with a black goatee—is missing. And so is Alia's—a striped one. And we wondered if you'd seen them. We heard you pick up stray cats." Oops. I instantly knew that last line was the wrong thing to say.

Albert Greely's sad eyes focused in on me. All of a sudden a look of recognition formed in them. And they steamed with anger again. "You're the feed store girl, aren't you? Your parents own the feed store."

I gulped. I nodded. I almost passed out.

He came down the two steps off the back stoop. "Your parents are in a conspiracy to hurt my business."

"No, sir. No, not at all."

"Yes, they are. They know I raise cats for a living. And yet they offer them free. I can't under...." And then he stopped. He put his arms to his chest and slumped down to the step.

Jason grabbed him from behind. "Dad, quick, where is your nitro?"

Albert Greely patted his shirt pocket. Jason got out a small vial and gave his father a pill. "Put this under your tongue, Dad. It'll be okay. Just relax. I'll call Mom."

Within minutes Albert Greely seemed to calm down, and color returned to his face. Jason looked at Maria, Alia, and me and motioned for us to leave. We hurried our way out of the backyard, back around front, and through the gate to the street.

Once there, Maria crossed her arms and shook her head at me. "Gee whiz. Smooth move again, Sherlock. What's with you? Don't you know how to talk to people without badgering them? It's embarrassing being around you. I think I've had enough. Come on, Alia, let's find something else to do with our day."

Alia took a step toward Maria. I walked up to her. "Is that

how you feel too, Alia? Aren't you worried about your cat?" I asked.

Alia shuffled her feet for a moment or two. "I don't know, Annie. It's just that this is kind of getting over our heads. I'd like to forget about it—maybe let someone else figure it all out."

The lines between Maria's and Alia's words slowly sank in. They only really wanted to be friends with each other. They didn't really care about me or Shakespeare or the weird things going on by my house. The going was getting tough and they didn't want to stick with me through it. I was being dumped!

Maria grabbed Alia's arm and started to pull her away. "So we'll see you at school Monday...probably."

I just looked at them walking away. Leaving me alone. Without a friend in the world—or at least in Mountain Center. I pulled my Walkman radio out of my mini-pack and turned it on.

"Hello out there, mountain folk...this is Andy at K-O-R-N with the best of country in the country. In fact, I've got a great one for you today. And here it is...."

"Lonely...do you know lonely...she was my only...but now I'm lonely...."

Click. I turned it off. I didn't need someone to tell me that message. I'd already gotten it.

18

FINDING THE
ONE TRUE FRIEND

It was a long walk home. One reason was that I took the long way home. I couldn't see me following ten paces behind Maria and Alia all the way back through town, listening to sleeping bag and tortilla chip stories all over again. I thought about stopping by Grandma Rose's house, but was afraid I'd run into them. Instead, I ended up going past the school and the hospital.

I just couldn't understand it. Someone once said that to have a friend you have to be a friend. I thought that was what I was doing. I invited them overnight. We told ghost stories by the campfire. I shared my mystery with them. We even formed the After School Sleuths and came up with our slogan—SASSY—Sleuths After School Serving You.

What was I doing wrong? Maria said I talked too much. Well, how does a sleuth find out what she needs to know except by asking questions? They probably never read Nancy Drew. And they probably didn't take the group as seriously as I did. After all, they had each other. I needed the group to have them as friends. Otherwise, why would they want to be my friend?

I sat down on a bench in front of the hospital. The late afternoon sun was soothing under the fall breeze. I lay down on my side, propping my head up with my hand. A fluttering sound—like flipping flags—from the wind blowing the aspen leaves calmed me.

It seemed strange that a hospital could be a quiet place. An elderly lady pushed her walker slowly around a sidewalk that meandered through a small rose garden. Mom had said there was a wing for convalescent patients. A couple of nurses in hospital greens were on another bench near the rose garden. Another woman slept in her wheelchair in the sun.

To the left of the front doors was the hospital sign. It had open arms on it with the following wording:

> Western Mountain Hospital
> A Passion to Heal
> We're Here—And We Care

That's nice, I thought. *Real friendly-like*. There were certainly a lot of friendly people in Mountain Center.

I laughed. I imagined myself walking up to the emergency entrance, asking to be admitted. The nurse would say, "Yes, miss, how can I help you?"

I'd answer, "It's an emergency—I'm dying!"

And she'd say, "But...but you look fine. What exactly is your problem?"

And I'd put my hand over my chest and say, "It's my heart."

And she'd say, "And what's wrong with your heart?"

And I'd say, "I don't have a friend in the world and my heart is breaking into a zillion pieces."

I laughed again. But then all at once the laughing turned into sobbing, and I sat up and turned away from the lady in the rose garden and the nurses on their coffee break and the woman in the wheelchair. I closed my eyes.

Oh, God, are you out there? All I wanted was one true friend. Grandma Rose said you know how I feel. I guess you'd probably know everything about me. I mean, you are God!

I've always believed in you—known you were out there somewhere. But Grandma Rose says you can actually live in me. That's what I really need, God. I need to know someone is there for me all the time. Will you come into my life, God? Will you come in and be my One True Friend?

I peeked open my eyes. Everything still looked the same. The lady was pushing the walker around for lap two. The nurses were getting up from their break. The woman in the wheelchair was still dozing. The wind was still blowing in the warm sunlight. I sort of brushed myself off as I got up to walk toward home. I laughed again. I hadn't warped into another time or anything.

But somehow I knew things were different. Like my attitude, for one. I thought about the people I had met in the last few days. Albert Greely didn't seem scary any more: He was just a sick and worried old man. Newly and Princess weren't cult freaks: They were kind, yet misguided ladies.

Then I thought about Maria and Alia. They really had been pretty friendly toward me. They didn't have to walk me home from school. They didn't have to stay overnight at my house. And they didn't have to chase down spooky things in the dark with me. *Maybe I was pushing them away, God, instead of them leaving me.*

It seemed like I was home in no time. I called Mom at the store to see if she needed any help. Dad had returned and things were slow, she said, so I could stay home. Link and Jeff were finishing up the chores. I climbed the steep steps to my room, threw the dozen pillows off my bed, and flopped down on it. I just thought I'd rest awhile after a wild, long evening and even stranger day.

But God had other plans.

19

ANOTHER
BREED OF CAT

Swoooosh. Clunk. Swooosh. Clunk.

I rubbed my eyes and squinted. What day was it? It was light out. I looked at the clock: 4:35. It was still Saturday. And I'd been asleep about an hour.

Swoooosh. Clunk. Swoooosh. Clunk.

What was that? I rolled off the bed, walked to the balcony door, and opened it. I squinted. Something was going on over at the grandstand. The binoculars were still somewhere on the floor. I kicked away a layer of pillows. Underneath them was a layer of dirty clothes. Under a pair of jeans I found them.

I focused in on the grandstand area. Someone was moving dirt with a big tractor thing. That was all. I scanned the racetrack. Nothing seemed out of the ordinary...until I focused on someone standing on the bottom row of the grandstand.

Tyler! What would he be doing there? Maybe he did have something to do with the strange goings-on. We had crossed Princess and Newly and Albert Greely off our suspect list. But Jason and Tyler definitely were up to something.

I left the door open and reached for the phone. I had to call Maria and Alia. I was a little afraid they would think I was obsessed by the whole mystery. And I was a little nervous that they'd even talk to me at all. But I figured that their friendship was worth the risk of looking silly. So I called Maria first, and her mom said she was still out with Alia.

I had to decide whether to go to the fairgrounds by myself. But first I thought I'd take one more look to see if Tyler was even still there. I walked to the balcony threshold again and peered through the binoculars. Things were out of focus now a little, but it seemed as though several figures were in the grandstand. I turned the knobs on the binoculars, stepping forward off the threshold to clear up the view a little when....

Squeak! *Oh, no! I knew I should have told Dad about that balcony.* I tried to grab for the door, but it had fully opened into my room. Crack! The boards melted under my feet and soon I was whooshing down the metal roof of the front porch. In the one second I had to put my brain together I thought of one thing: the rain gutters! I flipped to my stomach and as I reached the end of the roof, grabbed for them.

But I'd forgotten one thing. We didn't have rain gutters! Thud! Ouch! I landed in one of the big juniper bushes right in front of the house. I'd only actually fallen about six or seven feet off the roof, but the bush was prickly, and my arms were all scratched up. The bush was flattened. And Mom had said you couldn't kill junipers!

I brushed myself off. Other than some soreness and the scratches, I was amazingly okay. And somehow, I still had the binoculars around my neck. But from the ground I couldn't see past the shrubbery that stood in the way. I hobbled up to my bike which was propped against the side of the porch and headed off down the road.

In a few minutes I had entered through the pedestrian walk-through at the main back gate. I zipped past the animal barns, the chapel, the schoolhouse, and the gazebo. I dropped my bike and hobbled through the turnstiles at the grandstand. Then I walked up the cement stairway to the grandstand and peered through the binoculars again. The figures were at the far end.

Along with Tyler were...Maria and Alia? Huh? Why would they...? I scratched my head. Could they have been involved with Tyler and Jason from the beginning? That didn't make sense. But if they had been, that would have been a mean trick.

I had to know. I walked slowly toward them. Suddenly Maria spotted me and pointed me out to Alia. Alia motioned for me to join them. So I started to run, but then wanted to appear cool—you know, not too anxious—so I just sort of strolled—quickly—looking at the scenery and the big trac-tor moving the dirt around and the scenery again.

"Hi," I said as I approached.

"Hi," Maria and Alia responded on cue.

"Hi," Tyler said. "Did you come to watch, too?"

"Watch?" I asked. "Watch what?"

He shook his head. "My dad, of course. See? There he is." He pointed to the man in the big tractor.

"No," I said. "I just wondered what all of you were doing here. Is there something going on here I should know about?"

Maria laughed. Then Alia laughed. I wasn't sure if they were laughing at me or if I should have been laughing with them, so I didn't say anything.

Maria cleared her voice. "We sort of felt bad about dumping you like that, Annie."

"Yeah," said Alia. "So we stopped by your house. We knocked, but you weren't there."

"I was taking a nap." I bit my lip. "But what are you and Tyler...."

"We saw something going on over here, so we decided to check it out. It was just Tyler watching his dad, on his new dozer."

"That's why I came over too," I said. "When I saw people, I thought something might be going on with the fire or the cats."

"Fire or cats?" Tyler scrunched up his face.

I couldn't stand it again. Even if Maria and Alia walked away from me forever, I had to know if Tyler had anything to do with the fairgrounds mysteries.

I breathed in deeply. "OK, here it is, Tyler. There have been some weird things going on here at night—campfires, lights. And there've been some cats missing around here—my grandmother's and Alia's and others. And I heard you and

Jason talking about fires and cats the other day at the Frosty. And...and...so what's the deal? What do you know about all of this?" I held my breath.

Maria laughed. Alia laughed. Then Tyler laughed. Something was going on. I certainly didn't get it.

I put my hands on my hips. "Okay, so what is so funny?"

Tyler cleared his throat. "Annie, this is my dad on his new CAT. CAT—that's short for Caterpillar. It's a D5 Caterpillar dozer. He's doing a contract job for the county here on the fairgrounds today. But normally he's a logger. This is the CAT he picked up the other day from Oregon."

Maria was giggling. Alia was giggling. They'd already found out. Soon I was giggling. "You mean this is the cat you were talking about the other night?"

Right," said Tyler, "And I don't see what's so funny. This guy who works for my dad wrecked the other one at a logging site. It rolled down the mountain. And you'd better believe he lost his job." He stuck his hands in his jeans pockets.

"You mean, he got *fired?*" I said.

Tyler nodded. "And I don't think this is all that mysterious. I will never figure out how you girls think. I will never understand you. Nope. Never. Nope. Never." He walked away, shaking his head.

The three of us continued to giggle. In fact, I laughed so hard I thought I was going to fall over. So I sat down on one of the bleachers. And Maria and Alia joined me.

I looked at Maria smiling at me. And then I looked at Alia smiling at me. And all of a sudden something occurred to me. They had come over to my house to apologize. And they had decided to sleuth out the case. I was wrong. They really did want to be my friends!

I smiled back. Somehow I knew God had orchestrated this whole afternoon.

Maria broke the mood. "There's just one thing, Annie."

"Yeah?" I said.

"If Newly and Princess don't have anything to do with these mysteries.... And if Albert Greely and Tyler and Jason are clean, too...."

"Yeah?" I said again.

"Then who...."

I looked around. She was right. Who else could have a reason for taking cats and doing weird things at night on the fairgrounds? It seemed we were back at square one. At least on the case. As far as the friend thing went, though, I figured the After School Sleuths were a triangle—and a pretty solid one, at that.

20

CASING OUT
THE CULT

As we sat in the gazebo in the middle of the fairgrounds, we agreed to take an oath of loyalty to be true sleuths. In fact, we group hugged on it.

After the group hug, we agreed that only one suspect remained in our case. The cult. And we agreed that if we were going to be true After School Sleuths and live up to our SASSY motto, we had to muster up every ounce of guts we had and check out the cult firsthand.

"F-f-firsthand?" Alia asked, biting her nails.

"Firsthand," Maria said.

"You just took an oath, Alia," I said.

"Okay, okay, okay," said Alia. "I'll muster every ounce of guts I have and check out the cult thirdhand."

"Thirdhand?" I asked.

"Thirdhand," said Alia. "You'll be firsthand. Maria will

be secondhand. I'll be thirdhand. I'll be there...right behind you guys."

I shook my head. We agreed that since it was getting sort of late in the day, we needed to act fast, so they'd run and get their bikes and meet me at the feed store. The bikes would help, anyway, if we needed a fast getaway. That would give me a chance to see if Mom needed help feeding or cleaning the animals.

A couple of minutes later I was at the store. *Hmm, the Free Kittens sign is up,* I thought. *But the cage that normally would hold them is open. And no kittens are inside.* I leaned my bike up against the haystack in back, entered through the large, open shop door, and walked into the store through the back way. A woman was approaching Mom at the counter.

She wore a dark blue business jacket and skirt with a peach-colored silk blouse and pumps so pointy high-heeled that I thought they could be classified as lethal weapons. Her razor-cut dark brown hair zigzagged around her face and accented the sharp features in her face—dark eyes, short but pointy nose, well-lined eyebrows. This was a woman who meant business.

Then why is she holding three kittens? I thought. Moms in jeans with three begging kids in the car were usually suckers for the free kitten displays. Not well-dressed business people.

"Do you have a box or something for these?" she asked, half-smothering the wiggling gray-striped ones in her arms.

"We have cat carriers and cat beds and may even still have a used cage for sale," Mom said. "Is that what you mean?"

"Heavens, no," the woman said. "Just a box—maybe one with a lid. Just to get them home."

Mom shook her head. "Sorry. We just took a load of boxes and things to the dump. She tapped her fingers on the counter. "We don't lend out our carriers. I hope you understand. But we could hold the kittens for you for a day, until you can get something to transport them, Mrs... I'm sorry, I don't think we've ever met. I'm Kate Shepard." She held out her hand.

"Joanna Bentley." She shook my mom's hand, just about strangling the kittens with the other arm. "I own the new bookstore in town—the New Thought Bookstore. It's just that I need to transport these kittens, but I don't want to mess up my BMW. Maybe if I could just have a paper bag?"

"Paper bag?" My mom and I both said together.

My mom noticed me for the first time and stepped out from behind the counter. "Uh, Mrs. Bentley, this is my daughter, Annie. Annie, Mrs. Bentley."

"Paper bag?" I said again. "You can't carry those kittens home in a paper bag. That's...."

"I know," Mrs. Bentley said, "they won't stay in the bag. But maybe if I could borrow your stapler. I could just staple the bag closed and...."

"Stapler?" Mom and I said together.

"Excuse me, Mrs. Bentley," Mom said, "but these kittens are not going home in a paper bag, free or not." And she reached out and grabbed the kittens from her.

"Well, fine!" she said, stomping her high heels like a spoiled little girl and fire lighting in her eyes. "This is not going to go well with the evil spirit. And he will curse this business. It'll happen. Just you see." And she turned on her toes and marched down the aisle and right out the door, slamming it behind her.

I reached for the kittens and Mom gave me two of the three, which by now were all mewing in confusion.

"I don't get it," Mom said. "I thought it would be a neighborly thing to do—offer a place for people to put their kittens up for adoption. But first the cat breeder throws a fit and now this! What do you think brought all that on?"

I stroked the kittens. It was obvious that Joanna Bentley didn't have any affection for those kittens. No, she wanted them for some purpose other than companionship. New Thought Bookstore? That sounded kind of peculiar—maybe even something that would cater to cultists. And just maybe Joanna Bentley was a cult member herself. And what was that stuff about the evil spirit? And a curse? Was that for real? I knew I had an important lead. And when Maria and Alia rode up, I knew we had a hot suspect to trail.

21

A PRAYER FOR PROTECTION

"And where are you going?" Link caught my jeans belt loop with his hay hook. He and Jeff were resting on a couple of hay bales.

"Bike riding," I said, pulling away, "with my friends. Maria and Alia, this is Jeff. He works here."

Alia and Maria smiled. But they inched backwards and gave me the eye-raising, let's-go look. So I reached for my bike and was turning it around when a man in a small, rusting tan sedan drove up right in front of Link and Jeff. He didn't look like the typical hay customer which usually drove pickup trucks or four-wheel drive vehicles. His back faced me as I began to walk away, but he had a familiar walk, so I paused to figure out who it was.

"C'mon," said Maria, waving. "Let's go."

The man, dressed in brown coveralls, walked up to Jeff.

"Hi, son. What time did you say you were getting off work?"

Jeff looked at Link. "Five-thirty?"

Link nodded.

The man took off his dusty Giants baseball cap and smoothed back his speckled and thinning black hair. "Okay. That'll work. I've got a couple of leads on some places to stay. I'll pick you up then."

"Okay, Dad." Jeff turned to Link. "Don't we have to unload those feed sacks?"

"Yup, let's get to it." Link motioned to Jeff and the two went back through the large shop door.

The man put his cap back on as he turned toward his car, then noticed me and nodded with a smile of recognition. And then in an instant I knew him too. He was the groundsman at the fairgrounds—the guy who cut the lawns and did other odd jobs. Hmmm. The groundsman was Jeff's dad. I smiled back. Coincidences probably happened a lot in small towns. It seemed like everybody was related to everybody else. Even Maria and Alia said they were second cousins once removed. Whatever that means.

When I told Maria and Alia about what Joanna Bentley had done and said, Alia screeched on her brakes and came to a sudden stop. So Maria and I screeched on our brakes and came to a sudden stop.

"Girls," she said, "I don't know how you feel about prayer. But I'm going to pray. Right now."

I'd never seen this side of Alia. She was flushed with anger. And she was in charge! I'd always thought she was kind of wimpy. But there she was right on the main highway with her eyes closed. And talking to God!

"Oh, God, we need your mega help. In Jesus' name I bind Joanna Bentley or the evil powers she calls upon from hurting any of us or any of the Shepards or their store. Wrap us with your powerful protection and keep all of us safe. In Jesus' name. Amen."

I looked at Alia. She certainly was not the scared girl I thought she was. In fact, she seemed to have a lot of strength. I knew then that Alia must have a personal relationship with God too. I made a mental note to talk with her about that and maybe even visit her and Grandma Rose's church sometime.

Maria was staring at Alia, looking her up and down like Alia was standing there naked or something. "Alia, we've known each other a long time. But this is a side of you that I've never seen before. We've got to talk about this, girl."

"I've been meaning to," Alia said. "I guess I was just chicken."

"Well, let's get going," I said. "To the New Thought Bookstore!"

The New Thought Bookstore was right downtown between Mountain High Theater and Crowley's Antiques. I hadn't really noticed it before, but Alia knew right where it was. But as we coasted up, we saw the clock sign hung in the door:

Closed - Will Return Monday

The clock hands pointed to 9 o'clock.

"Gee whiz!" said Maria. "I was kind of looking forward to this."

I parked my bike and walked up to the front windows. "Well, I guess it's safe to snoop around a little. She won't be back until Monday."

The glass door stood a few feet back from the sidewalk so that it was protected from the weather elements. Above the door was a half moon with words painted over it:

Everything you need to enhance your spiritual quest

On either side windows displayed books, tapes, and crystals.

"I do not get this crystal stuff," I said. "I mean, a crystal is just a piece of rock. How could anyone think there was any power in a piece of rock?"

"Yeah, pretty dumb," said Alia. "These people are all mixed up. *God* is The Rock. A rock is not God."

All of a sudden as we were staring through the front door a shadow grew up and over us and soon we were staring in the glass at the dim reflection of...Joanna Bentley! I gulped. I think the other two did too, but my heart was pounding so hard I couldn't tell.

"Snooping around, Miss Shepard?" she asked coldly. "Or are you on a spiritual quest?"

We slowly turned to face her. She stood there, tapping her deadly weapon shoes and blocking the whole entryway with her presence. We tried to inch past her to the right, then left, then right, but she shifted her weight each time, so there was nothing to do but stand there and shake in our tennis shoes.

"Umm, no," I said. "Actually, we're on a cat quest. Alia

here has lost her cat and my grandma has lost hers. We're just looking all over town for them." I paused, looking at her steely dark eyes for the first time. "You wouldn't have seen them, would you?"

She backed off a step. "No, I haven't. That's odd, because I need a couple of cats."

"You mentioned that in the store," I said. "Exactly what do you mean, you *need* them?"

"I have the raunchiest case of mice infestation you can imagine," she said. "They're chewing on my books. They're ruining my inventory. Why, I can't even put out moon cookies for my customers. Those brazen things sneak up on the counter behind my back and munch on them too."

I looked at Joanna Bentley. She was a tough bird. She was looking me straight in the eye, and her eyes didn't waver. Her mouth didn't twitch. She seemed sincere. I mean, who could make up a story like that about moon cookies? But still I couldn't quite trust her. Was this the same person who talked of an evil spirit and a curse? How could someone change so quickly? Strange!

"Well," I said, "we were worried. I mean, we read that story in the paper about possible cat sacrifices and...and, have you heard anything about something like that going on?"

"I've heard rumors," she said. "I don't personally know anyone doing anything like that. But it's possible. There are *evil* influences anywhere."

With the word *evil* her eyes seemed to flicker—dart here and there. And then she looked up, thinking. But she bit her lip, as though she had thought about saying something, but held it in.

"I wouldn't get involved with that if I were you," she said. "It's for real."

Maria pursed her lips. "As real as talking to a crystal and it talking back?"

"No," Joanna Bentley said, "it's real. Believe me."

We walked away, keeping our eyes on our backs while we pushed off on our bikes in silence. Was Joanna Bentley another dead end? Or was she just a beginning? I sure didn't know. But I did know that I didn't feel comfortable around her. Or the New Thought Bookstore. But I didn't feel scared...or alone either. I knew God was with me, and so were my two friends.

Even so, we peddled like crazy out of there.

22

PHOTO FINISH

I made the executive decision to return to the feed store. From there, I figured, we could part ways. Maria and Alia followed me. It was was about six o'clock and close to dinnertime, and as much as I hated to call it quits for the day, I think we all knew we'd been licked. The only thing left, I figured, was to watch the fairgrounds for some new development.

Link was taking in the outside displays when we rolled in. "Hey, Squirt, make yourself useful and pick up some of the litter around here. Mom has already gone home."

Brothers! They sure knew how to embarrass you in front of your friends.

"We'll help, Annie," said Alia, tapping down her kickstand with her foot. "Let's see who can get the most!" *Trying to make up for how they dumped me earlier,* I thought. That was okay. I appreciated the help. Maria and Alia spread to different corners of the small parking lot, while I picked up trash blown in from the highway near the building.

"One more!" Maria shouted, running.

"I've got it!" said Alia, reaching for a folded-up piece of paper near the hay stack.

I walked over toward them with trash in hand to compare piles when....

"Eeeeehhhhhhhhhh!" Alia screamed, pointing to the paper.

Maria grabbed the paper from Alia. "Eeeehhhhhhhhhh! Quick! Annie! Look!"

I ran the last few steps and looked at the paper in Maria's hands. "Eeeeeehhhhhhhhhhhhh!"

It was the half photo, half drawing of the unknown woman! "Where would this have come from?"

"If the wind blew it in," said Alia, "that would be too spooky for words."

"No," I said, "it's folded neatly three times—like it could have fit in someone's pocket. More likely it was dropped. But who could have left it here?"

"Joanna Bentley?" said Alia.

"Or one of your customers?" said Maria.

Link slowly closed the big side shop door and locked it. "See you at home, Squirt." He walked over near me where I was standing by the hay truck. Beeeeepp! A tan car zipped by on the highway, the driver honking. Link waved. "Jeff," he said under his breath. He shrugged his shoulders. "Pretty nice guy, actually...too bad he's homeless."

"Homeless?" I said.

"Yeah," Link said. "He says they've been camping out—he and his dad. Probably down near the river—that's the only campsite nearby. Hope they got that apartment just now."

Jeff? Homeless? It was a wild guess, but I had a hunch!

I grabbed for Maria's and Alia's trash. "You guys won," I said, dumping the stuff in the trash can. "C'mon, we've got to beat it back to the fairgrounds. Now!"

They looked at me quizzically, but jumped on their bikes just a beat after I did. We raced down the highway, through the sidestreet, then down Fairgrounds Road. A few minutes later we were approaching the fairgounds. I scanned the area quickly and spotted the same tan car parked just outside the back gate. I motioned a follow-me sign to Maria and Alia, and we all zipped through the pedestrian walkway. Jeff and a man were just sitting down with take-out food at a picnic table under a shady tree right next to the barn marked "Beef."

Maria and Alia got off their bikes just as I did and walked up to me. They were giving me the *huh?* look. I nodded at them and motioned that they follow me over to Jeff. I took a deep breath and a hard look at the man. I was right. The man with Jeff—his dad—was the fairgrounds maintenance man. Just as I had suspected.

The man stood up. "You girls need something?"

"Oh, Dad," said Jeff, "this is the Shepard girl—Link's sister. Is it Annie?" I nodded. "Annie, this is my dad, Robert Holton." Both Jeff and his dad took off their dusty Giants caps.

"Uh, hi." I took a deep breath. "These are my friends, Maria and Alia."

Everyone smiled around and said hi. I knew it was my turn. "We, umm, found this on the ground near the feed store...and we, umm, wondered if it could be yours."

I pulled the photo out of my pocket, unfolded it and held it in front of me.

Robert Holton rubbed his forehead and sat down on the bench. Jeff reached out for the picture. "It's my mother," he said. "We found it hanging up in a coffee shop downtown. We couldn't figure it out—we thought we'd...."

"Burned it?" I finished.

"Excuse me." Robert Holton stood up and started walking away toward the maintenance shop building. "I've got some work I could do."

I looked at Jeff who was still looking at the picture. He tried bending back the creases and brushed off some dirt. "I guess Dad dropped it."

Maria stepped forward. "I finished off the picture," she said.

"We found it in the campfire," I said. "We were trying to figure out who was camping at the fairgrounds at night. We just live up the hill behind the grandstand."

Jeff smiled just to respond. He shook his head. "We hadn't figured on that. We didn't think anyone lived nearby. Pretty stupid, huh?"

"No," I said, "it's hard to see our house from the fairgrounds. And you just needed someplace to stay. You know, you should have told someone. This is a small town. People are friendly here." I smiled at Maria and Alia. "Someone could have helped you out."

Jeff sat down on the bench and Maria, Alia, and I sat down on the grass next to him.

"My dad's a proud man," he said. "He's been depressed a lot lately. My mom—the lady in the photo—her name was Sandy. She committed suicide two years ago. She was ill a long time. It was terminal, the doctor said, and she couldn't stand it anymore. My dad fell apart when Mom died. He couldn't hold down a job. We've been drifting around California since then, living out of sleeping bags."

I picked at a piece of grass. "But he got a job here awhile ago?"

Jeff nodded. "The week before school started. It was perfect timing. But we didn't have the deposit for an apartment, so we had to wait until he got his first paycheck." He cracked a smile. "We just found a place and get to move in tomorrow. It needs some cleaning up, but it's going to feel good to sleep inside. I'm sure sick of camping."

"That explains the campfires," Alia said, "but didn't you say you saw mysterious lights at night, Alia?"

"Yeah, I'd see a light here and there at night—sometimes late."

Jeff picked a splinter off the picnic table. "Dad hasn't been able to sleep well at night. Sometimes he goes off and just walks around the fairgrounds. What you saw was probably his flashlight. He just needed to be alone...to think. He's never wanted me to go with him. It's been hard. He really loved my mom."

I took a deep breath again. Partly to summon a little courage. But partly also to hold back the tears I felt forming.

"This may sound a little weird. But we've been hearing cats meowing. But we never see any. Do you?"

"Shortly after we moved here, we heard rumors about some strange group sacrificing cats. Well, Dad's never been crazy about cats, but Mom loved them, and he couldn't stand the idea of somebody doing something to hurt them. So when we found a stray, we picked it up and brought it to the grand-stand. We have about a half dozen of them there. They keep the mice down and they're nice company for Dad. They remind him of Mom."

"But if he loved her, why did he burn up that photo in the fire?" Maria asked.

"He has some mood swings sometimes," Jeff said. "One night he got mad at her for taking her life like that. He wishes she'd lived just a little longer—so he could tell her he loved her and stuff like that. He was angry, and so he threw it in the fire. I knew he regretted it when we saw it hanging at that restaurant, and I...I took it when he wasn't looking and gave it to him later. Boy, we sure wondered how it had gotten there."

Maria, Alia, and I sat there a few minutes just picking at the grass and throwing it. Jeff stared into space, biting his lip. We could hear a clank-clank coming from the maintenance barn. Jeff's dad was hammering something pretty hard.

We asked Jeff about some of the places he had lived. San Francisco. Sacramento. Reno. Work was hard to find. Alia invited him to her church. In fact, she invited all three of us to her church.

And we asked Jeff if we could look at the cats to see if

Shakespeare and Stripes were there. Sure enough, they were. They didn't seem all that excited to see us. I guess they kind of liked it there: The mice and Robert Holton's extra goodies kept them fat and happy.

I invited Jeff and his dad to dinner at our house. I knew Mom wouldn't mind when I told her the whole story.

Mom? Ohmygoodness! It was dinnertime, and I had to get home!

23

PARTNERS

"Can you believe it, Annie?" Maria said. "We've solved our first case." She was swinging on our porch swing with Alia. They had stopped by after dinner. They hadn't called or anything, but somehow I knew they'd stop by.

"Pretty cool, huh?" I was sitting in a nearby white wicker chair. I zipped up my hooded blue sweatshirt. It was colder right then than it had ever been in L.A., and winter was still three months away. But somehow I didn't seem to mind it.

Link and Jeff were sitting on the front porch steps. Jeff and his dad did come for dinner. Meatloaf—Mom's quick company fix. Mom is pretty good about having company over—always has been. She says it's important to be a Good Samaritan—whatever that is. She, Dad, and Robert Holton stayed inside to talk. It turned out that Jeff's dad and my dad had both gone to the same high school. Jeff's dad is about five years older, but they knew some of the same people. Small town coincidences.

Alia pulled her sweatshirt on too. "So what are we going to do? Hey, look! Here come Tyler and Jason."

We walked over to the steps and swung our feet over the porch railing.

Jason walked up to us, pointing to the balcony. "Hey, what happened there?"

Tyler laughed. "Bet it was a cat burglar." Everybody laughed.

Except me. I crossed my arms. "Oh, I just...I discovered a quicker way to get off to school in the morning."

There was a moment of silence. Then everyone laughed again, louder.

"Yeah, we all wish we could have seen that, Annie. Dad has threatened to hammer shut the door again. And Mom says she's going to have to replace this juniper bush here. Annie flattened it."

I rubbed my backside in remembrance of the moment. Everyone was laughing again.

"So I see your dad's got a new piece of equipment, Jason," Link said.

"Yeah," said Jason, "and I get to operate it once in a while. It's got a rops, a safety cage, so Mom says it should be safe."

Jason, Tyler, Link, and Jeff continued to talk about graders and dozers and other equipment. Jeff was kind of into that sort of stuff lately since he'd learned how to operate a forklift at the store. But the subject matter was not exactly my favorite, so I motioned Maria and Alia back to the swing. All three of us sat together, with me in the middle. We pumped our legs slowly.

"So I think we should get T-shirts that say 'AFTER SCHOOL SLEUTHS: SASSY' on them with our phone number," said Maria.

"Yeah," said Alia, "and put signs up around town, so people can contact us."

"Contact us?" I said.

"Sure," said Maria. "For other mysteries."

I snickered. "Other mysteries? In this town? I mean, this was probably some freak thing. Nothing exciting really happens here, does it?"

"Eeeeeeehhhhhhhhhh!" It was a woman's scream!

I jumped up. It couldn't be...could it? "I wonder if that's...."

Maria and Alia stood up, looked at each other and smiled.

"I wonder where my Chevy is tonight...."

I sighed, shaking my head at my silly partners. I knew we were friends, but I wondered if I'd ever learn those crazy country songs. *Oh, well...maybe by the time we solved the next mystery. Which is happening right now?*

Maria and Alia grabbed me by the arm. Together we rushed down the road. We'd find out soon!